Deceit

DEZAREE MCMILLER

Deceit
Copyright © 2023 Dezaree McMiller

Books may be purchased in quantity and/or special sales by contacting the publisher, Dezaree McMiller, by email at author.dezaree@gmail.com.

First Edition

Published in the United States of America
by Dezaree McMiller

Table of Contents

Acknowledgements

I found writing to be an escape from the reality of the world around me. In my darkest moments God placed on my heart to pick up a pen and paper and write and I am thankful. I am thankful that God has given me a gift to create characters and form a story to entertain myself and future readers.

I am thankful for my sister, Samiya McMiller, and spouse, Danial Otts, because they listened to me as I created this story and brought the characters to life. Thank you for patience and encouragement throughout this journey.

Although my son Elias Otts was a handful while editing this story, he encourages me to reach all goals so I can be a role model for him. Elias, I hope I can continue to set examples of what it means to reach your fullest potential in life.

Special thanks to my editor, Tanisha Stewart. With your guidance, I was able to take this story to the next level. Thank you for taking the time to answer all my questions. Thank you for your input and suggestions. All your hard work is appreciated.

Deceit

Chapter One

Aaron looked down at the shivering man on the ice rink known as the prison floor.

The smell of rust and chilled body odor crept into his nostrils as he listened to the familiar prisoner.

"Son?"

The man dressed in a beige one-piece jumpsuit with a number printed on the chest began to plead for his freedom.

Aaron ignored his pleas. "Don't call me that."

"I wanted to be there for you and your mother," the cold man chattered. "But I didn't know how." Tears formed in Aaron's father's eyes. The guilt from impregnating Aaron's mother and leaving her behind to care for their son made him feel worse than the tight shackles he was chained to.

Aaron stood frozen, glaring at the man who sported dark bags circled around painfilled red eyes. Aaron's heart palpitated, sending his respirations on a race to keep up. He clutched the photo he was holding in his left hand. Aaron studied the picture often as a teenage boy, embedding the memory of his father in his cerebral cortex. He often wondered what his father was like. As a child, Aaron hoped to have him more in his life to teach him how to be a man. Unfortunately, life didn't turn out that way. As Aaron became a man, his only connection to his father was found in the sleeping hours of the night.

Shackled to the floor by his hands and feet, Aaron's father looked back into his son's unforgiving eyes.

"Son - please, why are you keeping me locked up here? I have no food or water, and I'm cold." Aaron's father continued to beg.

Aaron raised his eyebrows and walked toward the prison bars. For a moment, he pitied the man and regretted having him shackled as if he was some slave. Aaron walked swiftly to where he sat chained, giving his father no personal space, looking down at him like he was nothing more than the ground he walked on.

"Did you care when you left my mom and me without food?" Aaron ducked closer to meet his father face to face. "Or clothes and a pot to piss in? Where were you? Why should I care?" Unable to restrain his anger, Aaron reached through the bars and punched his father in the face.

"So, you're going to be just like me?"

Aaron paused with his fist midair. His father's words pierced his soul, keeping the next blow to his face from connecting.

"Huh, son?" Aaron's father spit blood from Aaron's blow to his face.

"I am nothing like, like...." Aaron chanted, stunned by his father's words. Aaron started again. "Like..."

"Aaron, wake up!"

Aaron jolted out of a deep sleep, looking around and then focusing on where he was as he sat on the side of the King-sized bed to look at his iPhone.

"Shit!"

He scrolled through his missed calls.

"Faith, faith, faith." Aaron rolled his eyes. "Bri, Sativa Connect... Ahhhh, fuck!"

He murmured through heavy breaths, grasping at his chest. The missed calls and text messages from his women and connections made him feel urgent to move.

"You okay?" the concerned woman asked as she walked toward him.

"I'm good. We've been in this hot hotel too long. How much money did ole dude give you?" Aaron looked around, trying to see the money.

She returned a smirk as she twisted her Instagram model body toward the exit of the suite's bedroom and strutted to the bathroom.

"Aye, you suppose to have my money sitting on the table. Why the fuck is it in the bathroom?"

He wondered how often he repeated himself to Lupe, going over their hustle.

Aaron reached for his pistol and walked toward the bathroom. He scanned the room, looking for unexpected guests or men with wealthy net worths who returned for lustful seconds. After his quick trip around the Scottsdale suite, he went to the steamy, dimly lit bathroom.

"Chill." Lupe teased Aaron by repeating his lingo. She playfully tugged at his waist. "Celebrate?" Lupe hoped she could calm him with her suggestion.

Aaron looked at her with confusion as he clutched his pistol, intending to end her if needed. Aaron's light brown eyes locked with Lupe's green ones as she slid her black lace panties down her tanned honey booty.

The steam from the shower enhanced the smell of cherry blossom in the mist. The sensual look in Lupe's eyes invited Aaron to slowly release the tight grasp on his piece and reach out to touch Lupe's plump tits. Aaron traced the thin cloth that held Lupe's soft 36D cups. Lupe caught a sweat drip that began forming on his temple with a finger from her free hand and looked up into Aaron's eyes.

"I was getting ready." Lupe paused. "But your screaming...."

Aaron brushed her hand off his temple and looked away. Part of him felt embarrassed about getting so comfortable and falling asleep on the job.

"You know I can take care of you, baby," Lupe said, wrapping her arms around Aaron's long torso and laying her head on his chest. Lupe always tried sedating Aaron with comfort because she didn't like seeing him on edge. She felt a sense of guilt because she added to Aaron's anxiety.

"Oh yeah?" Aaron asked as he lifted her chin for their eyes to meet again. "Well, take care of me!" he ordered, whispering in Lupe's ear seductively.

Lupe silently nodded as an obedient submissive and gave Aaron all the money she made from her day's work. Women always gave in willingly to Aaron's demanding baritone. Lupe was no different as she got on her knees to invite him inside of her mouth. His thoughts returned to his real love as his dick relaxed in her warm wet lips.

His mind traveled to the money he was making, as well as his clothing brand, HEAT. HEAT expanded fast after he took a picture with an A-list celebrity during a SUNS basketball game and posted the photo on Instagram. He tagged the star and hash-tagged his HEAT apparel as always. The picture went viral after the celebrity reposted Aaron's picture. In an instant, the celebrity's IG followers and Aaron's followers liked the picture. This placed HEAT at the center of attention. HEAT's popularity grew along with sales.

Aaron pushed Lupe away. "Here's your cut. Get dressed so we can go. I gotta make a move."

Lupe's green eyes contracted as she caught her D-cups from slipping out of the thin cloth that covered her plump tits.

"Are you serious? The suite is paid for. Let's stay. Better than those trashy motel rooms."

Lupe snickered at Aaron as he scanned the room, stopped to look at the clock on the wall, and then back at his iPhone.

"Men of class are not paying for service in some trashy hotel in the Sunny Slope area." Aaron began to walk to the bed and put on his Yeezy Kicks. "You're right; you can stay, Lupe." In an exaggerated father-like tone, he added, "But you know the rules."

"We do the jobs, and we leave. We don't mix pleasure and business," Lupe chanted while rolling her eyes and getting dressed.

"Chill with the attitude, and...?"

"If I take care of you, you will protect me," Lupe said, shoving her last bit of business attire in her bag so Aaron's watchful eyes wouldn't notice.

"Right," Aaron said drily. "Let's go."

Lupe covered her 5'4 frame with a white lace Fashion Nova dress that hugged her Nicki Minaj figure. Lupe's ears sparkled with carats that the bathroom lights hit, making her shine as bright as the AP watch on her wrist. Her wet, thick, shiny black hair from the rushed shower fell down her back as she slipped her French pedicured toes into Christian Louboutin patent leather pumps with red soles. She picked up her Gucci luggage and iPhone quickly as she felt Aaron's burning eyes.

Lupe held her iPhone and keys in one hand and bags in the other.

"Let's go! I'm ready."

Aaron stood frozen as if looking into the eyes of a woman he didn't know. Before this moment, he hadn't seen Lupe dressed in designer from head to toe. He convinced himself she had been using the money they made to go shopping.

Lupe stared when she realized he wasn't moving.

"Aaron, you've been acting strange lately. What's gotten into you?"

"Who gave you all these designer bags and dresses?" Aaron demanded, eyeing her pumps. "I told you not to take any gifts, Lupe. That's trouble we don't need."

"These gifts are the least of our worries, Aaron, and you know that. I do my job, and you do yours. Besides, this dress is Fashion Nova, and it's a knockoff." Lupe held up her wrist and walked swiftly to the door as she spoke to him.

Aaron looked at her shoes to question them, but before he could fire back, his phone rang for the fifth time.

He answered with annoyance. "Yo, I'm on my way."

Lupe looked at Aaron, wondering who was calling him as they walked onto the courtyard for valet.

"Lupe, meet me for breakfast at eight to talk before we start our day," Aaron said as he closed her Nissan Maxima door.

"Si'."

***

Aaron entered his black, creamed, two-door Infiniti Q50 and drove onto Camelback Boulevard. He began to think about how much longer it would take to get the hundred thousand dollars he needed to keep his business in the luxurious desert outlet mall. He had already used up his resources from what his accountant and financial advisor had explained.

Fifteen minutes later, Aaron arrived at his East Camelback two-bedroom condo.

He shuffled through his keys, and as he began to open the door, it flung open.

Faith immediately sprang on him. "Where have you been? You said you were going to be here by eight. It's midnight!"

"I know what I said." Aaron exhaled from growing frustration. "I got caught up handling some business. Chill. I don't need this shit right now, and I'm tired."

Aaron looked down at the woman with a growing melon for a belly.

She looked back up at him, eyebrows raised. Anger and suspicion subsided as she began to feel a jolt of butterflies in her stomach.

"Why are you tripping? Be happy I'm here." Aaron looked down at the woman as he stood at the door. "Hello?" He waved his hand in front of the cranky pregnant woman. "Faith, here you go being weird again."

She grabbed Aaron's hand and laid it on her stomach.

Aaron's fingers trembled as he felt his unborn seed move from the touch of his hand. His eyes watered as he looked up at the ceiling while his father suddenly penetrated his thoughts.

Faith's voice broke his stupor. "I wanted to tell you I finally felt some movement from the baby."

Aaron quickly removed his hand from her stomach.

"Doctor Megna told me last Tuesday the baby's heartbeat was not as strong as the week before. I should have felt him move by now," Faith added as she followed Aaron on his heels. Before she could finish her words, Aaron slammed the bathroom door in her face. "You know I was scared to lose him," she whispered, shocked that he'd shut the door on her.

"Faith, get away from the door. Give me a minute!" he barked.

Faith knocked harder. "Why are you acting like this? The baby is okay. You're supposed to be happy."

"What was wrong with this baby anyway?" Aaron asked carelessly.

Faith rolled her eyes and began to explain. "I have placenta previa, where the placenta covers the birth canal, and I get painless bleeding. Dr. Megna said the placenta may migrate away. Until then, I should be on bed rest and see him once every two weeks to monitor our progress."

Silence separated Faith and Aaron for five minutes until Faith broke it.

"What the fuck, Aaron!"

"I told you to give me a minute. See, this is your fucking problem, all this nagging," Aaron barked through the bathroom door.

"I said the baby was okay. I'm not nagging." Faith groaned in disbelief at Aaron's reactions.

"You're still here?" Aaron asked, finally opening the door to talk with the pregnant woman bearing his seed. "I'm not speaking another language. Give me a fucking minute."

Aaron slammed the door again and locked it. Faith jumped back from the closing door, holding her stomach, confused and wondering what she had done wrong. She paced the floor and, within seconds, the grassy smell of burning trees enveloped in an apple cigar hit her. Faith remembered Aaron's text about finding a new dispensary near their condo.

"It has to be the placenta previa, or is it the bed rest or pregnancy? What is his deal?" she asked herself.

After ten minutes in the bathroom, Aaron sat at the kitchen table. Faith set a small plate of Cajun seafood pasta, a warm croissant, and a glass of lemon and water in front of him.

"I figured you might be hungry."

Aaron was silent but looked at his unborn child's mother as she continued.

"If you don't want to eat, I will." Faith tried to lighten the mood with her smile, showing her perfect white teeth.

"Make me a drink, Faye."

Aaron's irritation began to simmer with the taste of Faith's homemade meal. Despite his raunchy behavior, he began to think how she always knew what to do and when to do it to ease a stressful day. He looked at her growing belly as she poured the drink into his glass.

As Aaron finished his second glass of cognac, he reached into his pocket to pull out the cash he had made with Lupe today. It still shocked him how much money Lupe made for him. But it wasn't enough. He wondered what it would be like going all the way with her rather than slipping his dick inside her mouth. Shortly after his member was stimulated, his mind was bombarded with the thought of his business collapsing and a pregnant chick. The imagery turned him off from fantasies of Lupe. Besides, he was big on not mixing business with pleasure. Fucking Lupe would make things complicated, and his life was complex enough.

As Aaron swallowed the last drop and sat the cup on the dining table, Faith stood over him like a humble servant and began to pour another and watched him unwind. He reached out and took the bottle from her hand, thinking about the unfinished nut Lupe started back at the suite in Scottsdale. He pulled Faith between his legs.

Faith reluctantly fell into Aaron's arms and stared into his eyes.

He could tell Faith had noticed the wad of cash and was forming questions to ask him about it.

He kissed Faith on the cheek and then her lips, hoping to distract her from any questions she would ask him.

"You're not happy about the update?"

Aaron inhaled and exhaled the liquor, beginning to relax his growing anxieties.

"I need money, Faye. We don't need a baby right now."

Faith listened with folded arms in his lap.

"But the baby is here, so we gotta make it work."

Aaron's shoulders grew tight, and his lids uncovered the small vessel under the cornea of his brown eyes.

"How are we going to make it work, Faith? How?" He slammed his fist onto the table. "You are on bed rest because of this fucking baby. You can't work right now, and my business is hurting. Money needs to be made. I told you to get on birth control. You just finished college a year ago, traveling all over the valley for work. I thought that was what you wanted to do for a while."

"Three years ago," Faith interrupted, looking at the floor and shaking her head. "You don't pay me any attention. All you care about is money."

"Well, three years," Aaron said out of annoyance, shoving Faith from between his legs.

"All you care about is money," she repeated. "You have no values, Aaron? What about family? You don't love me. You never did."

Aaron's nostrils flared as he spoke his next words. "I'm talking, Faye, don't interrupt me. You be doing that shit a lot." Aaron shook his head. "Family or love don't put money in my pocket. I told you, you didn't need a nigga like me. You needed one of those lame niggas you went to college with. Shit ain't ever been good between us."

Their dog now stood next to Faith as Aaron continued his rant.

Aaron looked down at their Maltipoo and became furious.

"Yo, why didn't you take the dog to the groomer?" Aaron's New York accent intensified as his rage erupted.

"Bed rest, Aaron." Faith was getting pissed with his attitude.

"Come on, you take this bed rest shit too far. You're just laying around getting fat and ain't doing shit."

Faith flinched at those words, but calmed herself, trying to bring a sense of peace. "Did you forget we made plans for me to cook so we could chill together?" Tears formed in her eyes, and her plans for peace dissipated. "Oh, let me guess, you forgot because you're trying to make money."

Faith picked up the Maltipoo and headed to the condo's master bedroom. Aaron sat at the cherry oakwood table, poured another shot of cognac, and rolled his grass into his apple-enveloped cigar.

"Stop smoking in the kitchen!" Faith hollered in his head as he retrieved the lighter.

Aaron rolled his eyes as he continued to inhale his form of ecstasy.

As his high consumed his rage, he went to the master bedroom and watched Faith and the dog sleep in their California king. He began to think about how pregnancy looked good on her. Maybe his prior words were too harsh. Her brown skin glowed as the days passed, and her tits became plumper in the V-necks she wore to bed. The attraction he felt just by touching her rounded skin that shielded his unborn intensified his hunger and desire for cash.

***

"It wasn't always like this between us," Faith thought as she reminisced about the altercation between her and Aaron last night.

She continued to think of the fight as she prepared to leave the condo.

"Things flowed easily and naturally between us since we met. We never made things official, but we have always been each other's person. When we spent time together, it was always relaxing. Netflix and chill, going out for drinks, and long talks til the sun came up was the good ole days."

Faith tried to shake the intrusive thoughts about the good times she shared with Aaron. But just as she thought about the good times, the bad memories came full force.

"There were times he'd slip up and wouldn't keep his word. Leaving me dateless. It was fine. None of us was perfect. Until he fell asleep when we hung out, and I saw various women showing up on his caller ID."

Faith fumed. "This has always been an open relationship, and there must be someone else he's feeling. I know it!"

Faith was shocked by her realization.

Sweat bubbles formed on Faith's nose as she walked into the parking lot of her condo. Arizona's 102-degree forecast came to town to do its job, making Scottsdale unbearably hot. Her phone began to ring. Faith held Majesty close as she reached with her free hand inside her cluttered purse to grab her nonstop-ringing phone.

"Shit, this bet not be Aaron calling me. Oh, Hey, Chelsea!" Faith answered quickly. "I thought you were Aaron."

"Dang girl, I saw your post on Facebook last night. Is everything all right?" Chelsea asked.

"I'm good. What's up?"

"Uhm, nothing." Chelsea paused and lowered her voice. "I was just checking on you."

"Thanks," Faith replied, flustered as she gently threw Majesty in the passenger seat.

"Well, I'm gonna call you later. I'm busy right now."

Faith stared hard into traffic, blocking out Majesty's barks as she drove onto Scottsdale Boulevard. She couldn't shake the thought of Chelsea calling to check on her. She always tried to keep it together when Aaron blew up with his many fits. Hearing familiar voices from her friends and family from her hometown comforted her spirit. They demanded that she pour out her real emotions.

Majesty's barks grew louder, snapping Faith out of her trance.

"Okay, okay, I'll put the window down a little. Last time I let the window down, I almost lost you."

As Faith shifted to a stop at a red light, she couldn't help but notice the two-door Infiniti that mirrored Aaron's, even with the two-toned custom paint job. She was sure it was him.

"Hmm, the Breakfast Spot? Nah, he's at work. There's money to be made. Business is hurting." Faith repeated Aaron's words from last night's spat.

She circled the block to get another look at the car, making sure her assumptions were correct.

"Something isn't right," she said, looking at Majesty.

Majesty's ear raised as if to say, *I agree with you.*

"He probably got a new bitch." Faith was thick with disgust. She ducked and saw Aaron leave the restaurant with a woman behind him.

Faith sighed. "Nothing new."

Chapter Two

Breakfast was the most important meal of the day for Aaron. Various aromas from customers' food orders flooded the room. Aaron and Lupe sat at the table as they talked business, ate food, then left.

"Get in the car. We're going to our spot. Somebody hit me up trying to spend some money," Aaron said.

Lupe got into the car, slammed the door shut, put her phone in her purse, and folded her arms. Aaron looked at her, ready to blow a fuse, but he knew there was money to be made. He couldn't risk a petty argument getting in the way of making money from the freaky B-class celebrities of Arizona tonight. Aaron pulled up to the valet at Scottdale's Sunny Home Hotel and Resort and laid his hand on Lupe's leg.

"Look, I don't know what your problem is, but if you're feeling some type of way, I can bounce, and you won't hear from me again." Aaron paused, waiting for Lupe's response. "You knew what you were getting yourself into."

Lupe remained silent and stared out the window at her father and his men entering the hotel. They flashed their guns to assure her of her safety and arrival.

"See, this the shit I'm talking about, you on that weird shit again. I'm talking to you, and you ignore me. One of Khalid's boys said he got six racks right now, and I would give you more than half. Must be a concert tonight. But I guess I'll just go home, and we can return to our lives and be broke." Aaron fought to keep his composure. "Your choice."

A man dressed in a white button-up shirt stood at the window waiting to open Aaron's door. Aaron raised his left hand, gesturing for the employee to give him a moment. He took a drink of water, sweating from sitting under the 110-degree Arizona heat that pierced the tinted windows of his Infiniti. Even the blowing AC couldn't knock his anxieties about losing out on a quick couple of thousand dollars in exchange for some Lupe's pussy. Aaron looked over at Lupe and broke into a sweat, sensing she was not interested in last-minute business affairs that afternoon.

"What you gone do? Let's make this money!"

Another minute passed as Lupe stared into the Sunny Homes Hotel's lobby. Aaron shook his head, baffled by her disobedience. He made a mental note to set her straight later. The idea of the six thousand dollars offered for Lupe's services quickly interrupted his thoughts. Aaron pulled Lupe's hair from her face and locked eyes with her. She returned his glance for a moment but continued to stare back into the hotel, gazing at the men in the lobby. Aaron finally caught what had her attention and saw the men. She stared back.

"You know them or something?"

Lupe's thoughts about her parents and the shenanigans they made her a part of consumed her, not allowing her to answer Aaron.

"Daughter, I need your help," Brazo had explained as Lupe looked at him rolling her eyes.

"I am not getting in between you and Mom." Her Spanish accent flowed with every word she spoke.

"Your mom has threatened me with a divorce and to give the space at the outlet to someone else." Brazo shook his head and returned a concerned look at his daughter. *"Guadalupe, I am your father and will never hurt you. I need you to get to know this person. All I know is that he's a younger man. I need you to investigate further. What's his background? What does he want? Who is he?"* Brazo put his hands up and continued. *"He is a problem for this family."*

"But what does this have to do with me?" Lupe questioned her father.

"Just trust me for now. I will give you more details along the way."

She didn't want to do it, but knew she had no choice.

"Lupe?" he said, studying her with piercing eyes.

"Family comes first, and we have to stick together no matter what," Lupe stated.

As Lupe's memories came to an end, the question of how she got this far with Aaron came to mind. Lupe looked at her father and his goons, and she could feel Aaron staring at her and snapping her out of her thoughts.

"No!" Lupe said, finally breaking the long silence. "I don't know them," she added in a smaller voice.

"Can't fucking tell, what the fuck?" Aaron exhaled his frustrations.

When the men left the reception desk in the lobby, Lupe returned her attention to her cranky employer. She couldn't wait to be done with this.

Aaron leaned over to the passenger seat, invading Lupe's space, forcing his tongue into her mouth. He massaged his tongue against hers and gripped her tits with his hand, playfully erecting her nipples as he finished the kiss.

Just that quickly, she melted into him. Lupe hadn't planned to fall for her target, but she did, and she had fallen hard enough to reconsider her plan to cross him.

The only thing keeping her in place was the promise to her father.

"Let's make this move, and afterward, we can celebrate. Like you asked last night," Aaron said, still caressing her nipples and slipping his hand under her dress only to be met with a smooth pussy that excited him. Lupe looked into Aaron's eyes with thick breathing and touched his dick, which immediately awoke to her touch.

"Lupe, we can celebrate afterward."

"Let's go," she said without hesitation.

***

Aaron watched her every move as she retrieved her duffle bag from the trunk and spoke with the valet. He ensured he had his protection and even more bullets if needed. While Aaron told the valet driver not to scratch his paint job, Lupe was retrieving a key at the receptionist's desk.

Aaron's iPhone rang as he began walking into Sunny Home Hotel. The iPhone's caller ID read *Jay*. Jay was always there to listen and advise his friend in his friend's time of need.

Before Jay had a chance to offer his greeting, Aaron was already pissed again. Lupe had strode to the elevators without waiting for him. "Bro, this bitch acting mad weird." He spoke into his iPhone.

"What you mean, bro?" Jay asked curiously.

They had known each other all their lives, so Aaron spoke freely.

"Bro, when we work, we walk in together, and I make sure ain't nobody on no funny shit. But the bitch got a room key and went on the elevator without me."

"You think she's getting tired of tricking?" Jay paused, giving Aaron time to answer.

"Uh... I mean, yeah, but I break Lupe off damn near half."

"When y'all first met, she seemed like she liked you. Remember that night after the club at Quick Trip? Maybe kick it with her. That will put her in check. I mean, bro, she a baddie, and I ain't gone lie. You a lucky as hell, cause I'd-a been all in that!"

Buzzing sounded in Aaron's ear. He held the phone away to check it. "I just got a text from her talking 'bout *suite two-thirty-eight*."

"Aye, bro, y'all good, but look though, you always seem one step ahead of the game. I don't know how you're so clever. You got your hand in every hustle and niggas is hating."

"What's going on?" Aaron was getting heated by his friend's comment.

"Anonymous' IG page is posting your merchandise with *weak* written over it in bold red letters."

Aaron let out a hearty laugh and said, "What is this high school? Niggas is lame."

"You out here making a name for yourself, growing a fan base for HEAT. No wonder why some people out here are feeling threatened."

"Shit, man fuck it. I have to go. Stay up."

Aaron ended the call, wondering who was hating on his brand. He knew he was doing something right. He had people talking about him and his clothing line.

Everyone would soon talk about a store full of his merchandise once he finished getting his money right with Lupe. Once he got the amount he needed, he would be secure to rent his space at the Outlets.

Chapter Three

Lupe retrieved the room key and went to the assigned room without Aaron. She thought about how she wanted to get out of the game her father was playing but did not want to disappoint him.

When she arrived at the suite, Brazo planted a kiss on her cheek. "Guadalupe, my beautiful daughter, I missed you." Lupe's father was a green-eyed, olive-skinned, shiny black-haired Hispanic man.

"Dad, you have to hurry. He's coming soon."

"Si; have you been giving him the money, my daughter?"

Lupe raised her hand to her temple. "His attitude has me up here. Yes, Father, I can't wait until this ends. You all have to go because he's coming." Lupe waved her father and his men out of the hotel suite.

"Brazo, let's go. Teko has eyes on him. He should be getting off the elevator," Sam said as he held the earpiece to his ear and relayed the message.

"Don't forget, Guadalupe. Family first," Brazo reminded his daughter.

*****

Brazo practically walked into Aaron as Aaron entered the second floor.

"Shit!" Lupe said as she peeked out the door at Aaron and her father, barely brushing shoulders.

Aaron spotted her. "You know those niggas, Lupe? What the fuck is going on? You trying to set me up?" Aaron grabbed his protection and walked slowly toward her as if aiming at a target. He brushed past her into the suite.

"Come the fuck out!" he yelled, referring to the other two men who were with the man he had just seen near the elevator. "Lupe, you ain't gotta set me up." Aaron scanned the room and looked in every door, closet, and under the bed.

"Nobody's here, Aaron. I'm not setting you up."

Aaron studied her up and down. His gun was still cocked and ready to shoot if need be. He continued to survey his surroundings, sweat saturating his white and red Supreme-stamped shirt.

Once he saw that no one was in the suite, he went back to the door, poking his gun out first, then carefully looking at both sides of the hallway leading to the elevators. Once he saw that the men were gone, he fought to relax.

Lupe noticed his efforts and grabbed a cold towel from the bathroom, pulling him by his black ripped skinny jeans to the master bedroom.

"Relax, what's gotten into you?"

Lupe sat the cold washcloth on Aaron's forehead.

"What's wrong?" she asked.

Aaron remained tense. "Why did you come up here by yourself? You've been on some funny shit lately. I told you we didn't have to do this. I came into the Breakfast Spot this morning. You were in the restaurant talking shit on the phone. I haven't seen your car parked at your cousin's spot, and you got all this designer shit like you're up to something, Lupe. If you've been lying to me, I can bounce."

"No baby, chill and take off your shoes," Lupe insisted as she helped remove his Kanye West kicks.

"How did you know which room to come to and get the key?" he asked as he went into his supreme bag to retrieve his protection.

Lupe rolled her eyes and started to light the candles. "In case you didn't remember, we created my profile on the app together, and I can talk to the men one-on-one."

Aaron stood.

"So you have been side hustling. That's where all this expensive shit comes from. You're supposed to be getting your citizenship papers, your money right, and your own place."

"Uh... have you seen all the sick shit the president has been allowing lately?"

Lupe walked over to the bar in the living area and opened a bottle of cognac that was iced for Wednesday's meetings.

Aaron watched her every move, unable to relax.

Lupe continued, discreetly ensuring that Aaron could only see her back, not what she was slipping into the drink. "They're taking kids from their families, and it's like a prison camp for children. If Trump thinks he could strip my kids away from me, whether I had my papers or not, I'd be trying to off him."

Aaron stared at Lupe with tight eyes but swallowed the cognac as soon as Lupe put the shot in his hand.

"Can't wait to celebrate," Lupe said with a quick gulp of her shot, watching Aaron as he began to stretch his body on top of the King-sized plush mattress.

"What time is he coming? I don't want to get too comfortable."

"Three. I better get ready." Lupe began digging through her duffle bag with her back turned. She listened to him yawn and stretch, and he began to snore within minutes. Lupe tip-toed to where he was lying in bed and started taking up all his personal belongings. His iPhone, his wallet, and his gun. She carried all his possessions to the suite's living area and returned to the room to get her cell phone to call her father, Brazo.

As she dialed the number for her father, she looked over at Aaron to make sure he was breathing because his snore had stopped. Once she saw his chest moving up and down, she called her father.

"Hey, he's out. Move in."

***

Lupe swiped the phone to hang up, and the door inside the suite opened.

"Father, he was beginning to ask too many questions," Lupe said with irritation as she glared at him.

"How long do we have until he wakes up?" Brazo asked as his two loyal men entered the suite.

"At least three hours. The drug should be hitting his nervous system now. How long will this take with Aaron? I'm getting tired of his bullshit. His phone and wallet are there. I don't know what we're going to find."

Brazo could discern that his daughter was growing tired of their investigation and made a mental note to show her how he appreciated her with a gift.

"If you get what we need, we will have him signing over his space, or even his pitiful business, by the end of this week."

Lupe rolled her eyes.

"A person's life is in these damn things now," Teko announced as the phone began to ring. "Oh, shit, it's ringing now. Faith is calling. Faith has called twice already. Maybe a girlfriend, boss?"

"Maybe. Sam, make a note of Faith," Brazo ordered his other goon.

Sam retrieved Faith's number so he could trace her for information.

"She may be our answer to convincing him to sign over everything he owns."

Brazo trusted that the brothers Sam and Teko had found some way to get through to Aaron, as they had always found a way to get a task done in the past.

Brazo met Sam and Teko on Greenway and Grand Avenue in Surprise, Arizona, where men stood in a rocky open field waiting to be employed with work for the day. These men offered numerous sets of skills, such as painting, carpentry, and mechanical work. Teko and Sam could not legally work in the US. Brazo was opening his first restaurant with little to almost no money and needed help building his new restaurant, which was now a chain of restaurants.

Brazo's Burritos was a small, boxed drive-through-only building. It sat across from a high school in Phoenix, Arizona. Although there was no inside seating, the outside of the restaurant remained freshly manicured, with ample seating and a wooden fence with Brazo's menu engraved in the wood, separating it from other businesses in the surrounding area. He sold their signature, perfectly wrapped burritos that enclosed fresh ingredients from the farmer's market. Brazo's wife went to the farmer's market each morning before the day's opening to pick the freshest ingredients. The parents and teenagers from the local high school loved Brazo's food, allowing him to sell out of essential ingredients every night before closing.

***

It was rainy at midnight. Brazo and his wife had closed the restaurant, and Teko and Sam stayed to do some maintenance.

Boom! The cash registered was thrown onto the floor. Then there was a crashing sound, and windows burst with an object by two invaders.

"Cabron, are you lost?" Teko questioned a teenage boy as he grabbed him by the neck of his hoodie.

"How many are you?" Sam yelled at the other invader he dragged from the window as he tried to escape.

"I'm calling the police." Sam pulled out his cell phone but was interrupted, observing what his brother was already up to. He shook his head at Teko. "We can't revert to our old ways. Untie him."

Teko had the invader he captured tied to a chair. Hate was in his eyes as he moved on to Sam's captive.

"Teko, that's why we left Mexico. To do things the right way." Sam tried to reason with his brother about what he assumed he wanted to do to the teenagers for destroying the restaurant he and his brother had worked so hard to build.

"Call Brazo. Brazo can look them in the eye and make them pay for our hard work in this restaurant."

Brazo arrived at the restaurant five minutes after receiving the phone call from Sam.

"You thought you could steal from me?" Brazo's question filled the small restaurant as he stamped his handprint into the boys' faces.

"The next time either of you show up here again, I won't be so nice." Brazo chastised the two teenagers and let them go.

Teko and Sam needed work, so they offered to be security. Brazo agreed, and the brothers had been security for Brazo since the first restaurant. When Brazo was ready for an upscale restaurant and a luxurious outlet mall, their bond grew as strong as if they were family.

In Brazo's eyes, family came first. If someone tried to step in between, they got dealt with to send the message not to mess with his family or restaurant. Teko and Sam were always there to enforce the message.

Chapter Four

Faith prepared chips and dip to lounge on the sofa in front of the 65-inch smart tv, but a knock at the door startled her. She jumped, almost spilling her favorite snack. Faith slowly walked to the door, her legs turning into loose noodles. Her nerves were bad. With Aaron not answering her phone calls and random knocks at the door, she knew in the pit of her stomach that something was up.

"Why isn't he answering my calls!" Faith exclaimed while looking at her freshly trimmed pup. "Okay, calm down," she urged herself as she put her cell phone and snack on the marble kitchen counter island and walked over to the door.

"Who is it?" she asked, remembering she wasn't expecting visitors.

There was no answer. Faith opened the door, and there was a package that read *Aaron*. Faith picked up the package and walked to the sofa. She set it on the coffee table, wondering what was inside the mysterious white box. Without much hesitation, she opened it. Inside were pictures of outings with numerous women, text message records, background checks, and a particular image with *Faith* written in red marker.

Faith trembled with tears as she looked at the picture of herself leaving the hospital from the Prescott travel nurse contract in the emergency room that caused her order of bed rest. The memories of working in the Emergency Room as a nurse changed drastically as she fainted while caring for an elderly woman who visited the ER periodically. The memories overwhelmed her while she thought of calling Aaron to be by her side and him not answering because he was busy trying to open his store.

Faith rushed to the entrance of her condo and checked to see if the door was locked. She went back to the box and took it to the bedroom, pulling out her suitcase and packing her clothes. She held her phone in one hand while packing her overnight bag in another.

Her cousin answered on the second ring.

"I gotta get out of here, Tyler," Faith said through sniffles.

Tyler immediately jumped into action. "I'll be there tonight, and we will talk about it."

Faith hung up the phone.

She looked over the text message records and studied every picture with the different women, particularly the one with a Spanish-like woman with shiny black hair, olive-toned skin, and a perfect body.

"I feel like I've seen this chick," Faith said as she studied the picture more and more. Faith took pictures of everything with her cell phone.

"Fuck!" She began to pace the bedroom floor. "Should I call the police?" She paused and felt the baby move.

"Shit. I'm in trouble too." She ran inside the bedroom bathroom and began gathering more things. As she threw everything in the suitcase, one of the pages fell onto the floor with big black letters on the back.

Faith quickly turned every page around and put the pages together. They read, *Sign or Faith will pay.*

More tears streamed down her cheeks.

"If they're following him, they have eyes on me too. I can't drive to Las Vegas. They will follow me."

Faith thought for a few moments.

"Fuck it. I'll have to fly." She entered the closet and got one of Aaron's guns. As she grabbed it, she knocked over a pair of pants he wore last week that had another letter in the pockets.

Pulling out our percentage from your company. Your sales haven't met the agreement stated in our contract. Best of luck with your future business endeavors.

"He's losing the business, and now someone is threatening to take over?"

Something was not right. Although Faith knew something was wrong with Aaron, she was now involved. She knew calling her cousin Tyler was the best thing to do. Tyler was more than her cousin. He was her best friend, and they always had each other's backs. Faith shoved the letter in the suitcase, took the gun, and headed out the condo door to the parking area, looking both ways as she walked.

Chapter Five

Lupe took a shot of cognac to ease the anxiety from meeting with her father. She knew Aaron would wake up soon and wanted to be as relaxed as possible.

"Aaron, wake up already. It's time to celebrate."

Lupe held six crispy stacks of twenty-dollar bills. "Here's six thousand dollars!"

"Wait, I was sleeping?" Aaron looked around and reached for his iPhone on the side of the bed. He wiped away sleepiness from his eyes.

"Yeah, you lightweight. I tried to wake you when the client arrived, but you wouldn't budge. What if something happens, Aaron? How will you protect me if you're asleep on the job?"

He looked embarrassed for a second, then shook it off and said, "I thought we were celebrating, Lupe, not going over my job."

Lupe made drinks and sat on the bed in Victoria's Secret red lace panties and a bralette.

"It's all there. I counted."

Aaron checked the suite for any visitors.

"Starting that again?" Lupe giggled as she watched Aaron slowly scan the hotel room with a cocked gun.

"Damn right."

"Take the money." Lupe hung her head while she shoved the money into his chest. Lupe did exactly what Aaron wanted her to do. Give him everything. Aaron wanted every dollar, no matter how small the bill was. He kept his eyes on his money and his business. Aaron began scratching the back of his head as he looked into the iMessage app. Lupe stared with inviting eyes; as Aaron returned Lupe's gaze, he rolled his shoulders to release the tension that was building from Faith's text messages.

"Celebrate?" Aaron responded to Lupe's gestures to move on with their evening.

When he said those words, Lupe recalled the first night she met Aaron. They met at a Tempe nightclub.

Their eyes locked with lust, and an instant connection happened between them. Lupe brushed past Aaron as she tried to reach the bartender, then turned around, but he didn't take the bait.

"You'll regret not talking to me!" Seduction leaked with every word she spoke. He appeared unbothered, but Lupe wasn't ready to back down. She stared at him expectantly. "What are you waiting for?"

Aaron retrieved his double shot of tequila and lime.

He towered over her body, not giving her space when introducing himself. She knew expensive cologne when she smelled it. She bought her father the same DIOR brand.

"You're confident, huh?" Aaron paused as he looked at Lupe up and down. "Look, ma, if you want my attention, you gone have to earn it." Aaron smirked, took his shot, and walked away.

Lupe was speechless as she watched him walk across the floor. Men always fell under her spell until she met Aaron. Rejection was not a concept she mastered because she never had to.

Lupe grabbed his hand without thinking and asked, "Give me your phone?"

She put her phone number in his phone, although still in shock.

Fate somehow put them together again as they met at a local Quick Trip a mile from the nightclub in Tempe.

Her girls flirted with his boys, promising a nightcap together. His boy's ego couldn't turn down the possibilities with four assorted flavors of women. That night Lupe thought she made a real connection with someone, but money soon became the highlight of their relationship.

Lupe shook her memories away as she returned to where she had left the drinks and took a sip. Her father crept into her thoughts as she sipped the alcohol, and guilt arose as she thought that meeting Aaron was all a part of her father's game.

"It's all business, daughter. Put your family first." Lupe's father's words burned in her ears as she looked over at Aaron, whose eyes were glued to his iPhone, sipping his drink.

Aaron walked over to Lupe, embracing her, putting away the role her father instilled in her to play against Aaron and ruin everything he dreamed of. It wasn't just business for Lupe. No, she had a connection this time.

"Come here," Aaron commanded. As Lupe submitted into Aaron's arms, she couldn't help but think about how their business arrangement began.

***

It was Aaron and Lupe's second date, and they spent it at the Breakfast Spot he loved to eat at. Lupe sat at the bar, glued to her phone, swiping through a new app she had heard about. It was an escorting app that promised to connect women with wealthy men willing to pay for their time. She wanted to see if her ex-boyfriend was on there.

Lupe's thoughts continued to ramble on.

"What are you looking at?" Aaron asked.

Initially, she was hesitant to tell him. Still, she remembered he was under the impression that she had no money and was an illegal immigrant staying with a cousin. Lupe was drunk when she saw him that night at Quick Trip and told him a mixture of things she had seen on the news regarding Trump and that wall separating the US and Mexico.

"You're beautiful, Lupe." Aaron's voice was filled with charm after she showed him the app. "Shid, you and I can both use the money. You could make mad bank off that app, and we could split the profits, you know?"

Lupe was skeptical and didn't know what to say. Was he insinuating that she prostitute for him? A light bulb went off in her head. Her father, Brazo, could pose as a potential client and pay him out for purchasing the space in the outlet so that Brazo could put his restaurant in the area. She did it. She found a way for everyone to win without anyone being hurt. Lupe thought if her father could pay him back the money he had already paid to claim the store, he could move on safely without anyone getting hurt like the stories she had heard about her father's dealings in the past. Aaron would have his money back, so nothing of his was technically wasted. She felt bad that Aaron wouldn't get his brand HEAT where he wanted it to be. But her father's words of "putting the family first" quickly reminded her not to feel bad; she was doing what was best for everyone.

Lupe downloaded the app and created a profile with a pretty picture of herself and a list of interests.

She immediately received messages from strangers, felt excited, and couldn't wait to share her idea with her father.

***

Lupe could feel her temperature rise. Aaron's touch snapped her back from her thoughts of the day that brought them here. He dominated her in the moments they shared when she wasn't putting him to sleep with Midazolam. The Midazolam was her father's idea.

Lupe shared with her father that Aaron still needed money for HEAT's finishing touches before officially opening. Midazolam came after the escort app idea.

He needed a way to pass the time without Aaron realizing what was happening around him. Lupe overheard stories of what Teko and Sam would do to people who got in their way. The Midazolam syrup was harmless in comparison.

The drug was mixed in Aaron's drinks so Brazo's associates could drop off cash and figure ways to safely convince him to move on from the Outlets of Scottsdale Road. If Brazo's wife hadn't given the space to Aaron, the space would have been reserved for Brazo's restaurant, and Brazo resented Aaron for having HEAT where his new upscale restaurant should be. Nevertheless, it had to be done this way because Lupe was involved.

Chapter Six

Lupe and Aaron stood at the mini bar inside the suite. She looked up at him. He ran his hands through her ebony hair, watching her oval green eyes widen. The air conditioner broke the silence that fell over the master bedroom.

Lupe looked away, fighting the connection and burning with the desire to come clean. Aaron ran his hands through her hair. She felt as if she wasn't sheltered from the hundred-degree weather that emanated from the sun that rained over Scottsdale, Arizona. Aaron traced her hairline, sliding strands behind her ear, revealing the carats that pierced her ear lobe. Lupe caught his attention on the diamonds. Although she posed as an illegal immigrant, she refused to completely downplay her luxurious lifestyle. She simply didn't want to. She figured the escorting app was enough to be an excuse for her lavish clothing and jewelry.

Lupe redirected him by stretching her arms around his neck to bring him down to kiss her. He softly kissed her lips and used his hands to investigate her body for the first time. Aaron's hands traveled down her back as Lupe broke the soft kisses by breaking inside Aaron's mouth with the twist of her tongue. Aaron let out a soft moan.

"Mm."

Lupe's breathing grew intense as she listened. His moan sent her to a place she had never imagined with him.

"Thank you." Aaron took a deep breath. "I need to kick it with you," he said. "When we first met, you didn't have your green card, any legal documents for your citizenship, no job, or no way to support yourself. You were on that escorting app, and I thought that was a quick way to survive for the time being. I convinced you to do what you're doing now; ultimately, it would be worth it. I promised you I would take care of you, link you with my lawyer to help you get your papers in order, and make a lot of money with the escorting app."

Aaron took a sip of his drink and cleared his throat while Lupe listened silently, her eyes downcast.

"Things have gone as planned," Aaron continued. "You should have more than enough money for the lawyer, papers, and your spot. If we keep at this, you can maintain your place." Aaron's voice simmered as he switched gears. "I don't think no woman wants to fuck with random men anyway." Aaron shook his head at the thought of Lupe doing various sexual activities for clients in exchange for money.

Lupe's mind began racing as it seemed that Aaron was about to end their arrangement. She didn't want to let him go for more reasons than one. Her father needed her to finish the plan, but she couldn't deny the feelings she had for Aaron outside of that. "I'm almost there, but not completely," Lupe blurted, hoping it would buy her more time. "You're right, I don't want to do this forever, but I'm not in a position to stop yet. You said you would help me, Aaron. You said you would protect me." Lupe hoped that last bit would play into his guilt.

"You're right." Aaron sighed after contemplating her words. "But how I'm going to protect you if I fall asleep?" I guess I'm tired from stress with this fashion shit." Aaron rolled his shoulders to shake the ongoing pressure from his brand, HEAT.

Lupe was lost for words as she listened to Aaron say what was on his mind. She searched her brain, thinking of something to say to soothe his feelings. The last thing she wanted Aaron to do was to stop their hustle prematurely.

"You are doing your best, Aaron."

"I'm happy ain't nobody tried no funny shit," Aaron said as he took one last sip of his drink.

"Let's keep this going and see where this takes us; besides, I like spending time with you." Aaron was all about the money, so he nodded in agreement, and they continued their celebration.

***

The sincerity Lupe felt in her heart from Aaron's gratitude sent chills over her body.

The scandal of the prostitution act wasn't all her doing. Her father was behind this madness that would soon blow up and fall apart. But until then, she wanted Aaron in ways she never imagined. Aaron was different when not stressed or sobering from the side effects of Midazolam. He caught the attention of everyone anywhere he stepped foot with his 6'3 frame. Aaron was firm in what he wanted and believed. He was a smooth talker, making his swag unmatched and his presence contagious. At the same time, he was reserved and mysterious. He made every woman curious, and every hustler wanted to match his fly or join his team.

Until things came out, Lupe would soak up her surreal connection with someone who didn't know who she was and, most importantly, didn't fear her father.

Aaron's phone rang, reminding him to move to his next destination. Instead of doing this, he broke the number one rule to himself: Never mix business with pleasure. Aaron was always attracted to Lupe's petite body. She was everything he wanted Faith to be before she became pregnant with his seed. Lupe was surprised at Aaron ripping off her bra, but she had been anticipating this moment as he kissed her.

Aaron's thoughts of Lupe fucking other men couldn't bring his dick to soothe his lustful curiosities. But with the tension between him and Faith, he felt the urge to release anyway.

Aaron reached into his black ripped skinny jeans, pulling out a rubber.

"Bend over," Aaron instructed as she turned around to bend over. He slapped her ass, making her booty jiggle. Aaron enclosed his member with a skin-to-skin magnum rubber and slipped past Lupe's round booty. He exhaled as he felt the wetness that leaked from Lupe's pussy. He seared his handprint into her skin as he slapped her ass again. His knees grew weak and wobbly, and he could not maintain his posture.

"Shit tight," Aaron said with a stroke.

Duh, I'm not fucking anyone, Lupe thought and wanted to scream at Aaron but resisted and kept quiet.

After thirty minutes of pure satisfaction, he talked and laughed with Lupe as she tried to teach him a few Spanish words. Their conversation reminded him of how he would help Faith study Anatomy and Physiology while in college for her nursing degree at Arizona State University.

Faith's memories and humble beginnings reminded him of how much he loved and missed her as he drove home to his Scottsdale Condo.

***

"Baby!" Aaron chimed as he walked into the two-bedroom condo, kicking off his Kayne West sneakers. He unplugged one of his vapors from the Lenovo Laptop and took in a drag of concentrated cannabis oil.

Majesty wagged his tail as he greeted one of his owners.

"Baby?" Aaron questioned as he rubbed the Maltipoo's back. He looked at his iPhone and saw it was ten o'clock.

"She should be home."

Chapter Seven

Faith's flight landed at McCarran International Airport in Las Vegas, Nevada.

Tyler stood outside his all-white Trail Blazer SS, smoking a cigar and looking at the women who passed him. Once he saw Faith, his lustful look turned into a smile.

"What up doe, cousin?" Tyler greeted Faith with a half hug as he put her luggage and purse inside the truck's back seat. "You're pregnant?" he asked as he did a double take. "You didn't tell me." Tyler's eyes grew excited. "Wait til grandma and yo daddy see this!"

Tyler's excitement extinguished as he thought about how distant his favorite cousin and best friend was that she didn't tell him about her pregnancy.

"I thought we were better than this." Tyler stared, awaiting a response. "Why didn't you tell me you're with child?" Tyler asked this in his best impression of Rasputia from Norbit. He nudged Faith.

"It's Aaron's," Faith announced, watching the high-spirited Tyler turn flush with the news.

"You're still with him? I thought you left him alone a long time ago."

Faith rolled her eyes and folded her arms, sitting beside Tyler as they rode through the late-night traffic.

"You a damn doctor now?"

Faith returned to silence.

"What could you and Aaron possibly have in common? I mean, like, what does he do again?"

"Tyler. Damn. Okay!" Faith interjected, raising her hand to tell him to stop his rant about Aaron.

Tyler caught the growing annoyance of his cousin and decided to stop for now. He looked at Faith, appreciating that they could spend time together again. Their one-on-one time together was overdue. They kicked it like best friends, telling each other everything. He always admired his cousin but disagreed with her choice of men, particularly Aaron. Although he disagreed with her, he stood by her side. He listened to all the changes she went through with her relationship with Aaron.

Faith began to reminisce with Tyler about the time she and Aaron met.

It was September 2016, a hot summer month and the beginning of a new semester at Arizona State University.

The warm air burned Faith's skin as she left ASU's library at around eight in the evening. Faith walked as fast as she could to the first Uber she saw; a Honda Sonata. She didn't know that Uber did not belong to her. But Faith heard his voice, making her want to stay inside.

"What up," the Uber driver greeted Faith. His voice commanded Faith's attention at once. Faith dramatized the story as she exhaled and continued to reminisce with her cousin.

The song, Sevyn Streeter's *It Won't Stop*, featuring Chris Brown, played through the speakers as she shyly said hello back to him.

"I think you in the wrong Uber, Ma," he said.

Faith instantly flirted back, like second nature. *"No, I'm in the right Uber,"* she said with a smirk, moving her body wave bundles from her face. Once she realized she was flirting, Faith quickly became embarrassed and reached for the door to get out of the car.

"I'll take you where you need to go," he said with a smile and a sexy accent flowing through every word.

They talked during the thirty-minute drive to Faith's apartment. She learned where he was from, what he did for work, and about his daughter. Faith told him about school and answered every question he asked her, which was many. She could tell he was interested. She felt like she was on a first date with him.

Faith paused and looked out into the mountains, thinking of the first time she met Aaron.

She continued reminiscing with Tyler.

Faith sat in the back seat of Aaron's car, adjacent to him, to get a full view of his brown skin. She knew he was taller than her by looking at how his seat accommodated his stature.

Once they got to her apartment, he complimented her company, saying she was a breath of fresh air and talking to someone so intelligent was nice.

He invited Faith into the front seat of his car, and they talked all night.

"I couldn't take my eyes off his brown eyes." Faith paused again to reminisce about her first encounter with Aaron. She licked her lips.

Faith felt like she had known Aaron all her life, and she forgot she had just met him that night. She got so comfortable that she rubbed his arm while laughing at a joke he made and felt his peanut butter brown skin. Faith explained all this to her cousin.

Tyler interrupted. "What, you hungry or something? Girl, if you compare him to another ingredient. I know something..."

"I mean, I could always eat," Faith replied.

They laughed.

"But on a serious note, that one night led to many nights of vibing. We talked about our dreams and goals and took baby steps with one another to reach them."

"So what went wrong?" Tyler asked, sensing a change in his cousin's tone.

"He smoked weed and stayed out all night. I studied my pre req's and never went out."

Faith tried explaining their differences to depict that although they were different, they supported each other. "His clothing line, HEAT, started selling like crazy, and now he's trying to open a store." Faith hung her head to look at her stomach. "I guess this baby is just too much right now for him. My goals had a clear path, and his goals didn't. He's finally where he wants to be, and that's his focus. I get it, I guess." Faith finished her reminiscing that started excited and ended somberly.

"I don't want him to hurt you, Faith." Tyler exhaled, let his window down, and inhaled the cigar smoke. "He got to get his act right since there's a baby in the picture." Tyler pulled to a hotel, annoyed at his cousin's unusual silence. "So, what's up?" Tyler asked while helping Faith out of the Trailblazer.

Faith looked at Tyler with screaming eyes, unable to talk. Tyler could sense something was up.

Faith sat in silence at the restaurant table of the Vegas Hotel and watched her cousin inhale French fries as if he was a vacuum cleaner that sucked up food.

"I'm in trouble. Aaron got me mixed up in something," she blurted.

Tyler stopped eating.

"Trouble?" he questioned, wiping his hands with a paper towel. "What kind of trouble?"

Faith began to show Tyler the images she took with her phone and the letter she took from Aaron's pants. Tyler looked over everything, and his grey eyes turned blue as he stared at Faith and took in everything she was spilling to him. Faith sat there waiting for Tyler's response, trying not to interrupt. To Faith, what he had to say was precious and well-thought-out advice.

"Before I suggest anything, what the hell do you think is going on?"

Faith shrugged. "I think the investor who pulled out of Aaron's business is the one who is secretly trying to blackmail him and take over." Faith let out a long sigh. "I think they're trying to use me to get to him."

Silence fell between Faith and Tyler.

The waiter interrupted the two, asking if there was something else they needed, and Faith shook her head.

"Why, though? Why me?"

Tyler looked at Faith's round stomach.

"Aaron lays his head with you and that baby every night?" Tyler paused, gesturing for an answer.

"About every day, lately, now that I can think about it. He comes home, no matter how late it gets."

Tyler rolled his eyes.

"They must think his family is closest to that man's heart. Other than his money."

Tyler rubbed his chin as if he broke the code to Faith's mystery.

"They're threatening the closest thing to him."

"Damn, you might be right." Faith looked at her cousin in disbelief. "I should call the police." Faith stood from the table, pulling out her cell phone.

"No!" Tyler said, snatching the phone from Faith's hands.

"What the fuck!"

"We don't know the story for sure, Faith! Be easy. Besides, we from The D; baby, we got this."

Faith returned to her seat, staring at the evidence and feeling the growing anxiety that something was up and the urge that Aaron was in trouble.

"I want to help him, Tyler. I have an idea."

Aaron was her child's father and a friend she loved no matter what. She needed to be there no matter where they stood in their relationship.

Chapter Eight

Aaron sat on the sectional in his living room, thinking of the events unfolding in life. His mind drifted to the one person he wanted to be loved by unconditionally and to be there for him during this challenging transition in his life.

Aaron's eyebrows furrowed as he imagined his father. He shook his head to abandon the creeping thoughts that invaded his mind. But it was no use.

Aaron heard his father's voice.

"You know, son, you should be careful."

Aaron stood at the prison bars watching and listening to his father as he inhaled his cannabis oil. He shook his head and looked at his pen, wondering who was behind such a creation.

"Son?" His father continued to distract his attention from the cannabis oil.

"I told you about that word!" Aaron boasted through the bars of the prison cell that separated his father from him.

"Arrogance will soon blind you. You must step outside of yourself and pay attention.

Observe and listen, son. Consider yourself warned."

Aaron watched the shackled man who proclaimed to be his father, quietly wondering what he meant when he said that *arrogance would soon blind him*. Aaron had nothing as he tried to dissect his father's words.

Aaron watched his father relax his head on the cemented walls. The walls that once were cold turned warm and eventually grew hot, pushing his father from the wall.

Aaron jolted out of sleep, feeling the sun's heat kissing his skin.

Aaron looked down at the cannabis oil, convinced it was the oil's ecstasy making him dream of the man he had never met. He pulled out the only thing he had of his father. Aaron stared at his iPhone screen, observing the picture he had saved. He regretted thinking about the mysterious man. All he knew was a photo. He sat up on the oversized suede sectional and looked around. His subconscious reminded him of the sweet smell of cinnamon rolls that were usually baked in the morning. But that morning, there wasn't any smell of baked rolls or Faith standing over him asking if he wanted breakfast.

***

The living room smart TV displayed the time as eight o'clock.

"Baby?" Aaron questioned the condo as he walked the short hallway to the bedroom he shared with Faith. He ducked and scanned the room to see if she was there.

Aaron punched the air, realizing Faith never came home.

This wasn't like her. He became furious very quickly. Worry seeped into his heart as he thought about his girlfriend's disappearance. He retrieved another vape from the Lenovo to medicate his growing anxieties. Googled flights from Phoenix airport to Las Vegas, Nevada airport appeared on the screen along with the Bank of America account in another tab. Aaron took in the information, forming a story about where, why, and what might have happened to Faith.

His iPhone rang, distracting him from the valuable information he had discovered seconds ago.

"You straight?" Jay asked, concerned.

"I'm good, just getting up," Aaron reassured while giving a complete stretch and howling for a yawn.

"So, what's up? What happened with the Mexican joint yesterday?"

Aaron paused as he thought about letting his friend Jay in on what had been unfolding between him and his baby mama lately. He also knew something wasn't right with Lupe and needed a second opinion.

"Shit, I don't know, bro; she be acting weird sometimes. I walked into her rushing off the phone at the breakfast bar yesterday. She was talking shit."

Aaron began to pace the living room floor.

"Lupe had a key to the room, and everything was set up as if she had already been there."

Aaron stood still and rubbed his head.

"Shit sounds kind of funny, bro. I ain't gone lie," Jay agreed with him.

"Shit has been really funny," Aaron admitted. "Faith is gone. I think she's trying to start a new life with the baby without me in Vegas." Aaron shook his head and sat down. "Bro, she got racks in her account."

"Ain't your girl a doctor or some shit like that?"

Aaron paused as he looked at Faith's Arizona State University bachelor's degree hanging on the wall.

"Naw, a nurse," Aaron said, frustrated.

"You have been sleeping next to the plug." Jay let out a half chuckle. "You need to go ahead and marry her."

"Marry her?" Aaron questioned Jay.

"Bro. Have I ever steered you wrong?" Jay paused, giving Aaron time to answer. But Aaron returned silence.

"Look, man, we have known each other since the sandbox, and Faith ain't no Lupe, but she cute and got a good head on her shoulders. Just think about it, a'ight?"

"You a fool, bro." Aaron broke his silence.

"Look, I'm going holla at you in a minute."

Aaron sat on the sofa, gathering his thoughts, thinking about what he would do for the day and what Jay said. He valued his brother's opinion because they came from the same fatherless background. They had known each other since they were children. Their mothers were best friends and would support one another by babysitting for one another when needed. Aaron and Jay grew up to be more than friends. They grew up to be brothers.

He knew he had to show his face at the Outlets of Scottsdale Road, but he had to get his women and his money straight before he did so.

Chapter Nine

Aaron reflected about the conversation with his brother and decided to take his advice. He took his iPhone back out and dialed Lupe.

"Lupe, meet me at the Breakfast Spot," he said when she answered after a couple rings.

Lupe sang as she drove through traffic listening to *Boo'd Up* by Ella Mai.

She was excited to see Aaron this morning. It even crossed her mind that maybe she could come clean to him and they could be together. She didn't want to make a move too quickly though. She knew he could leave her altogether once she revealed anything to him, calling her a fraud. Or he could appreciate the information about her father's secret plans.

"Buenos Dias, Senor!" Lupe greeted Aaron with a kiss.

"You okay, Lupe?"

"Si," Lupe said while watching Aaron eat waffles.

"Good, I have been thinking...."

"Me too. I think we should be more than friends," Lupe blurted, surprising herself.

Aaron wiped his mouth with a napkin, glaring at Lupe as people around them clicked their plates with forks and knives.

"If I was going to be in a relationship, I could be with my baby mama. This ain't that, Lupe."

"Baby, mama?" Lupe repeated.

"Yes, baby mama, I have a baby on the way, Lupe," Aaron said coldly. "I need some time to think."

Lupe sat in silence as Aaron continued to eat his breakfast. Then, he suddenly stood.

"You out?" Lupe asked.

"For now, yeah. You don't need me. You look like you are doing pretty good on your own. You get room keys, designer bags, and shoes," Aaron said while looking at Lupe's feet.

"So what was yesterday?" Lupe asked, referring to them having sex.

"What about it?" Aaron asked.

Lupe became speechless. She was used to getting what she wanted from men. But Aaron was different, and this relationship was different.

Lupe laughed nervously, thinking about her father's instructions to keep Aaron under her watch.

"Aaron, you can't break things off with me," she said as she rearranged herself in her chair.

"Again, Lupe, you clearly don't need me." Aaron studied her attire.

"Fine, you will be back because you needed me!" Lupe insisted.

Aaron walked away from the breakfast table, relieved he had broken things off with Lupe and had one less situation to set straight.

***

Aaron reached his car, thinking about how he ended things with Lupe and Faith, and getting his life prepared for his unborn child. The breakfast spot was his favorite place to go in the mornings before starting his day, and he thought about what it would be like to start a tradition at the Breakfast Spot with his unborn child and Faith.

He cruised through the streets and began to reminisce about the first few encounters spent with his woman.

"Unfortunately, I have to work my second job at the Breakfast Spot to pay some bills. This nurse assistant work is not cutting it," Faith said into the phone as Aaron listened.

"Alright, look. I'm trying to see you, ma, so I'm coming to the Breakfast Spot in the morning, and you can serve me up waffles and eggs or something."

"It's a date," Faith agreed.

Aaron watched Faith glide through the restaurant serving everyone with a smile, making others laugh, all the while making him fall in love with how hard she worked. In order for them to spend time together, he would often have to visit her second job and order food as a customer. Her work ethic inspired him to work harder to accomplish his goals.

Aaron continued to cruise through Scottsdale and felt sorrow as he thought about how breaking things off with Lupe might have now tainted his Breakfast Spot visits. Aaron knew it had to be done but couldn't shake the image of Lupe's surprised look on her face.

***

Aaron walked into his condo while calling Faith for the third time and got no answer. He left a voicemail.

"Baby, pick up the phone. I'm worried."

Aaron stared at the phone after he hung up from leaving the last voicemail. He was blown away at how quickly the roles had reversed. Faith usually called him nonstop, giving an excuse that she was worried.

He walked into his condo.

"Faith!" he called out, hoping she had returned.

Silence except for Majesty, who ran up, wagging his tail.

Aaron went into the bedroom and lay across the bed, his father's words repeating in his brain like a hot knife through his soul.

"Arrogance will blind you, son."

What the hell is that supposed to mean, Aaron thought. He picked up the phone and called Faith again.

"Baby, I know things have been rocky with me lately, but I promise to explain everything to you. I know where you are. I was thinking with the baby on the way...." Aaron paused as he took a deep breath. "I think we should get married and do it right."

Aaron swiped the phone, hanging up, knowing he would get her attention with a proposal. All he could think about was saving his business peacefully and having more than enough money, even with an investor pulling out.

Aaron couldn't help but think about his childhood. The memories flowed through his mind unexpectedly as he thought about Faith and his unborn child. He never wanted to relive his uncomfortable childhood.

He remembered one day in particular.

"Baby, get ready you going to your grandma's. I know you didn't eat dinner, but your grandma will feed you." Aaron's mother had announced.

"Ma, you going to work again? It's boring at grandma's and all she will give me is a bologna sandwich with cheese that doesn't melt, water, or grits." Aaron pleaded with his mother.

"This fourth shift will put food in the refrigerator, Aaron. Now go into my room and get the car keys. I'm going to change, and we will go. I don't want to hear another word."

Aaron followed his mother's orders and looked for her car keys. As he looked for the car keys, he found a Polaroid picture of a man he'd never seen.

"He left us when you were a baby," Aaron's mother said as she watched Aaron study the photo.

"Is he my daddy?" Aaron asked.

"Yes, he's your father, and that's all you need to know. He left us with nothing when you were a baby without any explanation. He's not a good man and you don't need him. I don't want him to hurt you."

"What's his name?" Aaron asked curiously.

"I don't want you to get to know him and then he leaves you like he left us before. I'm only protecting you, Aaron, now let's go."

Aaron sat up on the bed, shaking his head to banish his childhood memories. He now had a new outlook on his situation. He would marry Faith, get his hands on that traveling nurse money, save his business, and be a father to his unborn.

He picked up the white box that lay beside him. His name was written on it. He must have been totally out of it because he never noticed it laying on Faith's side of the bed. It was partially hidden by the comforter; maybe that was why. He opened the box, stunned when he saw that it had revealed all his secrets. He jumped up, grabbing his gun as he read the message about Faith.

A million questions ran through his brain at once. Most importantly, did Faith make it to Las Vegas safely?

Aaron's entire world came crashing down. He did not play about his money, business, and plug to maintain it, which meant war for him. As he thought about his love for Faith, a tear dropped from his eye in disbelief.

Aaron was in his head. He punched the air and yelled to his condo. "I've been in and out of these hotels with Lupe! I could have been at the crib with my bitch working on some new designs for HEAT."

Aaron gathered his things; as he began to leave, he realized he needed to talk to his business mentor. The store was not open yet, and his open-for-business date was approaching soon.

Chapter Ten

Aaron surprised Teko and Sam with the unexpected move of seeing his business mentor.

"Yeah, boss, I got eyes on him," Teko said as Aaron walked past him to his Infiniti.

"I lost the girl." Teko let out a long sigh. He was ready to get the bad news out so his boss could order new ways for Aaron to give up his space. He hadn't actually opened the store, had he?

Teko sat quietly as Brazo screamed into the phone.

After a few moments, he cut into the rant. "Brazo, we got this...We can do this without the bitch."

Clat!

Teko closed the flip phone.

"I'm starting to believe this is not about taking over the space for the restaurant." Teko reached for his gun to off Aaron.

"What you doing, Teko?" Sam quickly grabbed his hand with the gun.

"I'm giving his family a reason to arrange a funeral!" Teko looked at Sam with eager hatred in his eyes.

"Woah, woah, woah!" Sam put two hands up to say stop.

Teko sat back in the driver's seat to calm his growing anger as his brother tried to talk him out of ending their investigation.

"Give me one shot, and I'll end this. What's the reason behind Brazo following this guy?" Teko exclaimed while pointing his Glock toward Aaron, who was starting his engine. "We are wasting time, Sam. Just shoot him, and we can eat carne asada tacos by six." Enraged by Sam's nonchalant behavior, Teko continued. "If he dies, he can't open the store, and we will be done babysitting." He spoke as if he had figured out a million-dollar answer.

Sam stared back with agreeing eyes. His brother was at it again, ready to put another man in the dirt who was in the way of Brazo's success. Teko grew impatient after weeks of following and watching Lupe whore around with Aaron.

Sam shook his head, disagreeing with Teko's reaction. "Let's not do it here, Teko."

Teko rolled his shoulders and shook his head to release the itch to kill.

Sam continued. "You're right, though. Why all the trouble?"

"Right time, Right moment!" Teko said, spreading a menacing grin as he drove behind Aaron's Infiniti.

Aaron drove one hour from his condo in Scottsdale until he reached Tucson. He pulled into a five-bedroom estate. Teko and Sam pulled a few feet down to watch their target's next moves. Sam grabbed his binoculars from the rear passenger seat. He stared, with binoculars in one hand and his trigger finger held snuggly to his hand-crafted gun with *Sam* written adjacent to the chamber.

"Who is this, Aaron... really?" Teko asked as he shook his head in disbelief.

"He knows Claudia?" Sam chimed in.

"A little too well!" Teko hissed back as they watched Aaron and Brazo's wife Claudia embrace for a long time.

"So, it is not just about the restaurant," Sam said as his mouth hung open, watching through the binoculars.

"They must be..." Sam began to speak but was stopped after observing Lupe's unusual behavior.

***

Lupe didn't expect to see Aaron's car parked in Claudia's driveway. So many questions ran through Lupe's mind as she ducked down into the bushes of the Tucson estate after leaving the pool. Was Aaron dating her mother? Lupe hid in the bushes on the side of the house, away from where

Claudia and Aaron stood but close enough to hear them talk.

"Take this as a learning experience and relocate your store, Aaron," Claudia suggested.

Aaron grew tense. "That's not what I want though, Claudia!"

Claudia sighed. "The Outlets are where anyone like you starting a fresh new business would want to be. It has a lot of foot traffic; the landscape is beautiful, and it's equipped with everything a shopper needs, and it caters to all ages." Claudia looked into Aaron's eyes with pity as she stroked his back, then she continued. "But I still think you should let it go. Investors are pulling out before your launch. That's a bad sign."

Aaron stood in silence, listening to her, annoyed by her comments about his brand HEAT but letting her finish.

"Can I come in?" Aaron asked as he continued standing in the Tucson estate's doorway.

"Guadalupe, my daughter will be here soon, and I don't want her to see you here."

"It's been a minute, boss lady," Aaron said as he grabbed her by the waist, bringing her closer.

"As much as I would love to take a ride," Claudia said with a wink, "You've gotten me into enough trouble." She handed a book to Aaron. "Dave Ramsey is going to take over for me now." Claudia could see the apprehension in Aaron's eyes. Claudia grabbed Aaron's penis and said, "I have taught you everything you need to know.

71

Dave Ramsey will have to take over. We can't see each other anymore."

"Why?" Aaron objected.

"You know why. I'm forty-six years old, and you are thirty; this just isn't right. Take a few days and think about what I am saying." Claudia paused to observe how he was taking in what she was saying.

"Start small with the clothing store. Look for a Glendale strip mall with space for sale in an area that is popular for people you want HEAT to gravitate to."

The door to the back entrance alerted the entire house that someone was there. Lupe had forgotten about the home security system as she tried to sneak inside so Aaron would not see her. Her family home was big, but because her parents constantly fought and she did not want to be a part of the fighting, she left home to live with her auntie and cousin in Phoenix.

"Guadalupe, is that you?" Claudia yelled to the house.

"Guadalupe?" Aaron repeated with a puzzled look.

"Yes, my daughter. You have to go, Aaron."

Aaron took the Dave Ramsey book and left the estate.

***

Lupe began pacing the floor, trying to figure out what to do or say. She wanted to confront her mother but didn't know what to say.

"She cheated with Aaron; I can't believe this!" Lupe said to her bedroom.

Many scenarios ran through her mind. Lupe felt disappointment, anger, and guilt for getting involved with her father's Midazolam drug drama. She knew not to fall for her father's enemy, who was her mom's now ex-boyfriend.

Before they began drugging him during her fake prostitution scheme, Aaron was different, much calmer. Brazo and Lupe were not doctors, so they always eyeballed how much syrup to give Aaron to sedate him. But Aaron's swag turned her on, and she couldn't resist. She understood why her mother left her father. Her mother was seven years younger than her father, and the attraction her mother felt for Aaron wasn't a surprise.

"Think bitch, think!" Lupe chanted as she paced her bedroom floor.

"Claudia," Lupe called out, annoyed by her discoveries.

"You're calling me by my name?" Claudia questioned as she stood in Lupe's bedroom doorway entrance.

Lupe stopped pacing and stood within arm's reach of Claudia.

"I heard you say you couldn't see him anymore?" Lupe asked as she stood with anger consuming her.

"No, Guadalupe, it's not what you're thinking. He's just an associate." Claudia tried reaching her hand out to calm Lupe. She could see Lupe was getting angry about her infidelity.

Lupe put up her hands to exaggerate her words, and her glare pierced Claudia's soul, not allowing her to dilute her and Aaron's relationship.

"Stop it, I know what I heard you say to him!"

Claudia's guilt for hiding her relationship with Aaron became apparent as she became teary-eyed and returned to silence.

Lupe yelled. "How could you do this to us? My father doesn't deserve this." She stepped closer to Claudia.

Claudia was taken aback by Lupe's behavior. She wiped a tear and sat on Lupe's bed.

"You weren't always around when your father came home late, or had unexplained blood on him after being with Teko and Sam." Claudia explained. "You didn't have to worry about what kind of trouble he put this family in constantly, and his lack of attention to me."

"I'm sorry I can't do this right now. Mom, I need some time to think."

"I understand." Claudia said as she left Lupe's bedroom.

Lupe sat on the bed, taking in everything Claudia had just unloaded. She sat still as she thought about her family's secrets and her feelings for Aaron.

Lupe's mind wandered to Aaron. She knew she had to face him soon. She was concerned that

Aaron had possibly seen her at the house. Did he notice it was her car in the driveway? She decided to wait to see if he contacted her about suspecting anything.

Chapter Eleven

After the third cousin of the family trio arrived, Faith and Tyler settled in. When Faith moved from Detroit to Arizona, it sparked Tyler to venture out of their Detroit hood to Las Vegas and the third cousin to disappear without telling anyone where he was going.

"What up doe, cuz," Tyler said as he shook hands with his cousin.

"I'm good, my baby. That four-hour flight took a minute. But I chopped it up with a fine bitch flying to Arizona. Shid, she helped pass the time."

Jeff looked over Tyler's shoulder to see how he was living.

"Shit, come in, big homie." Tyler noticed the curiosity on Jeff's face.

"Damn, cuz! This is what it's like in Vegas?" Jeff marveled as he gave himself a mini tour of the luxurious apartment. Jeff's eyes were big and round, while his mouth hung open as he wandered around Tyler's crib. "My nigga living well compared to the State Fair apartments back in the D." Jeff gave an approving head nod, and Tyler gave him some dap. Now that formalities were out of the way, Jeff was ready to get down to business. "So why the urgency for me to come to paradise?" Jeff looked out the window at the palm trees.

"You trying to smoke? I got some broccoli." Tyler gestured with his index finger and thumb like he had already had a blunt between his fingertips.

Without words, Jeff knew something was up and that he would hear an ear full over some rolled-up smoke and shots.

"Hell yeah! After that flight, I need some smoke."

Tyler put his hand on the rustic oak table, showing the broccoli and chilled Tequila.

"You got some backwoods and Don Julio!" Jeff rubbed his hands together and nodded in approval.

"Thanks for the coming, short notice and all." Tyler began to roll up his form of ecstasy. "Ya boys didn't hit me back, though."

Jeff looked at Tyler, offended. "I'm a one-man army. I work best alone." Jeff's eyes spoke *killer kid*, and Tyler knew his name was heavy in the streets of Detroit. He wasn't to be taken short of seriously. Though he was dangerous to outsiders, Jeff was kind-hearted to his family.

"Boy, fuck you mean, work alone? Sounding like Mr. Incredible and shit." Tyler lit his blunt and inhaled.

Jeff smirked, and Tyler let out a hearty laugh.

"Nigga shut yo ass up." He glared at Tyler, knowing he would have whipped someone's ass for the comment if it had been someone on the streets of Detroit. "Whatever problems ya pretty boy ass got will be lightweight."

Tyler stopped laughing before he had to do a boxing match with his cousin over the joke.

"I'm-a let Faith tell you what's going on." Tyler handed the blunt to Jeff, and Jeff inhaled the smoke.

"Aye, why do you call it broccoli?" Jeff looked at the blunt as if it was much more intense than the ones he'd had in Detroit.

"Shit, this that healthy green."

"Lame ass," Jeff smirked and stood as Faith entered the living area.

"What's up, cousin? Long time no see." Faith stretched her arms around the middle of Jeff's torso.

"What's up, Ms. Grey's Anatomy? Left the hood and became a doctor!"

Faith blushed and corrected him.

"A nurse."

"Same shit. But that's what's up, Faith - proud of you."

Faith's blush deepened, but Jeff was ready for business.

"What happened?"

Her smile was erased, and Faith told Jeff the short version of what had been unraveling in her life as she watched her cousin's smoke session from across the room. Their bond couldn't be broken. They were each other's best friends, except Jeff knew a lot about Faith and Tyler's lives, but they knew little about Jeff. He kept it that way with his family for safety reasons. The less they knew, the better off they were. Jeff almost caught a charge when he went to the playground with Tyler and Faith. Tyler and Faith were being bullied, and Jeff didn't allow them to stand up for themselves. After a kid pushed Faith onto the ground and then pushed Tyler. Jeff didn't allow Tyler to retaliate. He gave the kid an uppercut to the chin, sending him across the grass. The kid passed out from teenage Jeff's blow to the face. Since then, people in the neighborhood called him *the killer kid*, and the three cousins became inseparable.

***

Jeff couldn't get his words out as he stared at the pictures of the dirt on Aaron. "So, you fell in love with a disrespectful..." He looked up from the evidence and continued. "Arizona nigga." Disgust stretched every syllable he spoke.

Tyler interjected, "Brah, that's what I said." Faith cut her eyes at Tyler.

"You hear anything I said?" Faith asked Jeff.

"Yup." Jeff took his shot of tequila, seeming uninterested in Faith's dilemma. But he was serious about his cousin's safety. Jeff looked over to Tyler and said, "Lightweight."

Tyler shook his head. Faith looked between the two, confused and trying to figure out their inside joke.

"I'm-a have a word with your man when we get to Arizona," Jeff said calmly.

"For?" Faith questioned. Jeff's jaw tightened because of Faith's questioning. Faith took the hint, remembering who her cousin was. "Sorry. Just curious about what you were going to say to him. I don't want things to end badly." Faith thought about what she heard her cousin did to her aunties' boyfriend. Jeff's mother.

Jeff read the concern on Faith's face.

"He should be marrying you. You came a long way from running around with them hood rats on the eastside and making CNA money. Ya feel me?"

"Yeah, yeah," Faith replied, irritable.

"I don't know if it's the baby or that nigga who got your mind clouded, but you need to wake up."

"My man's Fly Bape, Pharrell Williams sneakers, Supreme...." Jeff added as he pointed at Aaron's Instagram picture he pulled up on his iPad.

Tyler and Faith looked over his shoulder.

"This nigga has up-and-coming new music artists and some B-list celebrities wearing his shit on IG." Jeff paused and looked back at Faith. "He plugged," Jeff said, convinced Aaron's name carried some weight in the music industry.

"I guess." Faith shrugged. "I really don't know for sure. From what I get from it, a new artist with many followers promotes his clothing brand along with their music."

"What is his little clothing line called?" Tyler asked, looking over Jeff's shoulder.

"HEAT," Faith answered.

Tyler and Jeff saw the upcoming artist wearing Aaron's branded dad hats and graphic shirts. They knew Aaron had some legit business to uphold.

"A'ight, we up!" Jeff exclaimed.

***

Faith, Jeff, and Tyler drove Tyler's Trail Blazer SS back to Scottsdale, Arizona, where the demise of Faith and Aaron's relationship deepened. Everyone rode in silence, listening to the sounds of the car stereo drowning out their unspoken words.

Faith looked out the window into the landscape of the mountains, thinking deeply to herself, *I just got the job of my dreams, travel nursing.*

She looked over at Jeff, obsessing over the pictures of threats, and thought, *Now I got my crazy fam with me to bring the heat where it's already hot.* Faith second-guessed bringing her family into the ordeal but knew there was no turning back now.

Jeff's light-hearted demeanor was demolished as he continued to study the pictures of threats made toward his cousin. He embedded every piece of evidence into his brain. It would come in handy when he caught whoever threatened his family.

Tyler continued to push the SS through the mountains as Nipsey Hussle's *Grinding All My Life* played through the subwoofers.

Faith watched her cousin drive like a pro through the mountains and around every curve as if he had gone this route many times. A part of her felt like she had never left Detroit, Michigan. Detroit was famed for its auto industry, getting its nickname the "Motor City" from the industry. Detroit had art and soul embodied in the heart of its streets.

But in the old school, if you woke up one morning on some foul shit, you were to be bodied by the hands of someone who didn't like the smell of your shit. Because of that fact alone, Detroit was also called the "Murder Mitten." Despite the palm trees, mountains, and college degree, Faith was the typical girl from Detroit. The only difference was that nobody she knew had died yet.

Chapter Twelve

Faith, Tyler, and Jeff arrived at the Scottsdale condo, ready to bring Faith's troubles to an end. Faith and Tyler settled into the apartment as Jeff explained that he would be in after walking around the neighborhood.

Faith unpacked in her bedroom then went to look for her cousins.

"Where's Jeff?" Faith looked around her condo.

"Come here."

Faith walked to the window where Tyler stood, pointing at the building identical to hers across the street. "He's up there."

"He's not going to shoot nobody!" Faith grimaced, putting her hand over her mouth and staring at Tyler for an answer.

Tyler could see the scary look on his cousin's face and said, "How could he if he didn't know who to shoot?"

Faith whispered, "I've heard stories at home." Referring to Detroit. "Jeff shoots first and connects the bodies later."

"Yeah, I heard that shit too," Tyler admitted, looking guilty.

Faith and Tyler's reminiscing was interrupted as the doorknob jiggled and the key turned to unlock the door. Faith wasn't expecting visitors and looked at the clock on the wall, knowing it couldn't be Aaron. He never came home before ten in the evening. Faith's phone began to ring, and *Unavailable* spread across her caller ID. Tyler drew his heat from his waistline, pointing it at the door. He instructed Faith to answer.

"Hello?"

"Ya fuck boy is coming in, Faith," Jeff said from the other end of the phone. "I got eyes on him, cuz." A red light beamed on Aaron's chest as he turned at a nearby sound, indicating he was a target. Aaron stepped back with his hands up as he noticed Tyler's gun drawn in his direction.

"This nigga ain't flinching. I guess he got some balls, huh?" Jeff joked into the phone. "Tell Tyler to put his gun down."

"Okay," Faith replied with a cracked voice.

Aaron knew from pictures and stories from Faith about her family that her trigger-happy cousins were here. And by the look in Tyler's eyes and the red-light beam on his chest, he knew they didn't come for a family vacation.

"Yo, Faye, you alright? I've been trying to call you!" Aaron said with his hands up, looking at her and hoping she would tell her family to lower their guns.

84

"I know," Faith said, glancing at her cousin Tyler. Tyler got the hint and lowered his weapon.

Aaron strolled to Faith with his hands out, embracing her. He looked at Tyler and said, "It ain't safe to be here right now, fam."

Tyler put his gun back on his waist. "Faith caught me up already. We ain't gone let nothing happen to her; she fam. The police ain't got to do shit for Faith's protection." Tyler's words dripped with authority because he only cared about ensuring Faith was safe.

"Know what I mean?" Tyler looked sternly into Aaron's eyes, then broke the stare off as he reached into his cargo pants pocket to retrieve his backwoods and broccoli.

"However, we gotta figure this out. Until then, everything is on me." Aaron pulled out a fat knot of hundred-dollar bills, peeled off ten, and handed the money to Tyler.

"Hotel and entertainment," Aaron suggested as he held out the money.

"Don't worry about it, fam. I'm not leaving Faith, so keep the money," Tyler insisted humbly. He returned all bills but one and said with a menacing smile, "I'd like to see what Arizona grass is blowing like."

Aaron nodded in agreement. Money was tight for him anyway. At the same time, if he had support to protect his family, no amount of money mattered to him.

Faith shook her head at her cousin's addiction and began to walk to the bedroom she shared with Aaron.

Aaron talked to Tyler for a few minutes, then went into the room where Faith sat on the bed, flipping through channels.

***

Aaron shook his head to rid his father from his thoughts. He rolled his shoulders to release the urge to blow off some stress. He wanted to roll up his form of ecstasy, but he resorted to cannabis oil. He could feel the thick tension between himself and Faith, and he couldn't help but feel guilty for what he'd been putting her through.

"Yo, you mad?"

"I'm good." Sarcasm dripped from Faith's mouth with her reply.

"Those other women didn't mean shit to me," Aaron said nonchalantly, referring to the box of secrets that still lay on the bed.

Faith looked at the box and then back at the TV, continuing to flip through the apps and quietly ignoring Aaron. Aaron could sense that Faith was not trying to hear him out, but he tried to get her attention anyway.

"So, your cousin can smoke in the kitchen, but I can't?" Aaron thought of the past scolding from Faith when he would smoke in their kitchen, and Faith lost self-control as she began to yell.

"He's a guest, and you're a headache, Aaron. If he wants to smoke, he can!"

Aaron's jaw tightened in surprise at Faith's outburst. As his anger grew, his father emerged from his thoughts.

"Wrong move, son." His father snickered, and Aaron shook his head as he tried to remove the unwanted visitor from his mind.

"So, you gone scream or talk to me like an adult," Aaron asked casually.

Faith was appalled by Aaron's words, and she looked in his direction, cutting her eyes at him because he was mocking her. She would say those exact words to him when they would get into altercations in the past, and all he would do was scream.

"There's nothing to talk about!" Faith spat.

Aaron's father resurfaced to interrupt his thoughts.

"She's in a mood." Aaron's father stood from his thin mat known as a mattress and walked to the prison bars, looking through Aaron's eyes. His father looked out into the world surrounding Aaron, yet he was limited to Aaron's subconscious.

Faith was watching a movie on Netflix, and the concentrated cannabis oil Aaron consumed woke up his love pole.

"Son, you gotta finish what you started earlier." As Aaron's father instructed him,

Aaron's mind began unraveling the Tucson estate events.

Aaron rubbed his love pole while sitting on the king-sized bed next to Faith. Aaron looked at Faith and locked eyes with her, demanding her attention. Faith became mesmerized by his brown eyes, so her gaze spoke desire. She was angry with Aaron but couldn't fight her hunger for him to be inside her. He hadn't been inside Faith since she discovered she was pregnant months ago. Her vagina began to pulsate as she looked away. Then she stared at his growing love pole that bulged under his Fendi joggers. He kicked off his Balenciaga kicks and sat his vapor pen down on the nightstand. Aaron reached over to caress Faith's cheek. Faith touched his hand and began to remove his hand from her face. She didn't want to give in to the sexual tension building between them. Aaron could read her defiance. He quickly enveloped Faith's hand with his and kissed the back of her palm. Aaron inhaled Faith's scent, filling his nostrils with her aroma. The smell of Versace Crystal was his favorite scent that she wore often.

Aaron kissed her lips, taking her by surprise. Faith submitted to the burning desire they felt for each other. She hungrily kissed Aaron back, wrapping her arms around his neck to embrace him.

"Hmmm."

Aaron forced his tongue into her mouth, and Faith moaned in excitement.

Kissing her with his tongue made her juices drip freely from her womanhood. Aaron put his fingers between her thighs, confirming what he already knew. He provoked her love box to cry for him. Ache for him.

"Damn, baby." Aaron's baritone, low, and deep voice sang. "You miss me, huh?" Aaron spoke seductively, pulling his V-neck over his head to reveal his chiseled chest. Faith planted kisses on the *rolled cash* tattoo on the right breast of his masculine chest. Her favorite spot on his body.

Faith suddenly stopped, and Aaron asked, "What?" noticing her hesitation.

Faith looked toward the door, remembering her cousin was in the living room a few feet from their bedroom. Aaron quickly figured out the reason behind Faith's hesitation. Feeling the swelling of his love pole, he switched the app on their TV from Netflix to Pandora.

Aaron pulled out his dick. He massaged himself while taking in every inch of Faith's body. Her brown skin glowed, and her visible freckles connected as her cheekbones rose from smiling at Aaron's visible manhood. She spread her legs, inviting Aaron into her love box.

Aaron spread her legs further and bent forward to taste her juices.

Faith gasped.

She moaned softly as she listened to the slurping sound Aaron made with his tongue against her clitoris. Aaron's tongue moved to the rhythm of Yuna Crush, featuring Usher. The song reminded Faith of the beginning of her and Aaron's relationship. A crush pulled her to become deeply involved with the man she wanted to spend the rest of her life with.

Aaron came up from his late-night meal between her thighs and kissed Faith, exchanging the taste of her love. As Aaron gave Faith a sloppy kiss, he pushed his love pole gently into her love box. He began swaying to the song *Too Deep* by DVSN, now playing from the app. Aaron moved his hips strategically to every spot deep within her womanhood that sent Faith into her own form of ecstasy. Keeping up the song's tempo, Aaron matched his strokes to the beat, but before he released his semen, he pulled his raw pole out of her box.

"Fuck. I missed you too, Ma," Aaron's baritone expressed.

Aaron lay back on the bed to give himself a second to relax, his dick growing anxious to explode from feeling the wetness of Faith's love. Faith stared at Aaron's dick that stood to the ceiling, and she climbed on top of him, introducing his love pole to her love box once again. But this time, her box enclosed the entire pole, allowing him to tickle her cervix.

Aaron helped Faith to slowly grind her hips on his pole to the melody of Daniel Caesar's *Best Part* featuring H.E.R. It was as if Pandora was a live DJ in their bedroom. Their personally orchestrated playlist connected the lovers again.

Aaron watched the tears form in Faith's eyes and wrapped his long arms around her body, pulling her closer to his body. Faith continued to grind on his dick.

"Aaron!" Faith moaned. "I'm about to cum. You feel so good."

Aaron could feel Faith's walls dilate and constrict, sending a shower down the skin of his dick. That commanded an intense release, followed by "Ahhhh!" a roar as if he was a lion in the jungle.

After they finished, they drifted to sleep.

***

Aaron's instincts told him the person in the kitchen wasn't Tyler.

"Yo son, wake up!" Aaron's father yelled in his brain. Aaron woke up and looked over at Faith, who was still sleeping. Aaron's stomach grumbled at the aroma of cooking food in the kitchen.

Aaron reached the spare bedroom and could hear someone in the bathroom. Aaron retrieved the gun he kept in the hallway linen closet top shelf and strolled toward the kitchen with it cocked. Aaron pointed his weapon toward Jeff, standing at the stove stirring chili.

"Put your gun down, fam," Jeff said as if he had eyes embedded in the waves of his fresh cut.

Aaron had never met Jeff, nor had Faith ever mentioned him, so Aaron kept his pistol cocked.

Jeff pulled two Glocks out and whipped around, pointing them at Aaron.

"I said put the gun down, fam," Jeff demanded through clenched teeth.

"Fuck is you?" Aaron asked.

Tyler entered the room, pausing between Aaron and his cousin. Tyler looked back at Jeff.

"What's up, fam?"

"The nigga walked in here with a gun, and I asked him nicely to put it down." Tyler could feel the thick tension between Aaron and Jeff but felt more concern for Aaron because he knew his cousin was on the verge of losing his patience.

***

Tyler and Faith witnessed Jeff lose his patience with a guy at the club one night. One night a chick walked up on Jeff and started twerking on him. She gave him her number and walked off with her girls. The chick didn't know her man was in the building watching her. He walked up to Jeff, knocked Jeff's phone out of his hand, and said, "Don't call my girl." The guy walked away and became lost in the club's crowd. Faith, Tyler, and Jeff left the club that night immediately after that because the guy had purposely knocked Jeff's phone out of his hand

and spilled his drink on Jeff's Gucci fit. The woman who gave Jeff a dance was outside, too, and she began to flirt with him again. After seeing Jeff and his girl's interaction, the guy started cursing at Jeff.

Jeff was a UFC replica, and anyone with eyes could see he cared for his body at the gym. Jeff executed one of his *killer kid* uppercuts, sending the man from the club clear across a car parked next to where Jeff stood.

***

Tyler got the hint, knowing his cousin wasn't patient if somebody didn't take his orders. Tyler lowered Aaron's gun, saying, "Ever had some Coney?"

Aaron didn't know what was going on but put it together that Jeff was family.

Aaron stood there, continuing to eye Jeff. "Yo, fam, I didn't know who the fuck you were."

Jeff withdrew his two pistols and turned the stove off. "Nigga sit down."

"Ain't no Coney Island at this muthafucka." Jeff was referring to Arizona's lack of Detroit restaurants.

"What you make, cuz?" Tyler looked at the stove as he sat on the kitchen island.

"Chili cheese fries," Jeff said with a grin.

"Shid, I'm trying to keep the weight off," Tyler said as he flexed his muscles.

Jeff gave Tyler a stern look.

"Let me make me and my man's here a plate." Tyler looked at Aaron, who was still puzzled by his new guests.

Tyler sat the Detroit-American Coney Island-styled food in front of Aaron. The plate of chili fries drizzled with shredded cheese and onions. Aaron's stomach grumbled at the food he would have never thought about eating. But the fries smelled good, and after the altercation with Jeff, he didn't want extra added beef over fries.

Tyler noticed the skeptical look on Aaron's face. "Bro, lighten up, shid; you just got cutty last night." Tyler looked at his smart watch, noticing the time.

Jeff cut his eyes at his cousin. "Yo ATL looking ass."

Tyler laughed, and Aaron smirked and forked his French fries, thinking of the lovemaking with Faith a couple hours ago.

Jeff and Tyler looked at Aaron suspiciously as Aaron ate the fries and swallowed. Aaron caught the looks of his guests and quickly regretted eating the food, thinking, *Yo, did these niggas just poison me or something? Why are they looking at me like that?*

Tyler laughed again, reading Aaron's mind.

"We ain't here to hurt you, fam. You got a seed you gotta raise, and we are here to help protect that." Jeff stood with his 6'4 frame towering over the table, with his fingers intertwined. "That's all, my nigga."

Aaron nodded.

"But I am going holla at you before I leave," Jeff said sternly.

Aaron nodded again as he stuck a fork full of fries in his mouth. "Yo, you ain't gone get nun like this unless you order some Carne Asada fries from the Mexican joint Faith has me going to up the street." Aaron said this to lighten the tension between Jeff and himself.

"Oh yeah?" Tyler took a mental note.

The fellas ate for the next sixty seconds, cleaning their plates.

Jeff spoke up as soon as he put his plate in the sink. "My nigga what's going on?" He crossed his arms and leaned against the refrigerator.

Aaron instantly knew he needed to come clean with everything. But he couldn't. He just got in good with Faith by making love to her, and she didn't need to know he resorted to his old ways of pimping. His secrets were in a mini box, but not all.

"Investor pulled out my company, and I think they are trying to blackmail me into signing over the store." Aaron paused. "Why, I don't know."

"You got some beef with some niggas you ain't settle?" Jeff questioned as if he was a detective on the case.

"Naw." Aaron shook his head. "I'm a businessman; I keep it cordial with everyone. Never know when you'll meet a critical connection or new business proposition." Aaron schooled his guest.

"I feel you, I feel you." Tyler, a businessman himself, agreed with Aaron.

Jeff wasn't buying the mediocre response and knew there was more to it, so he began to question more, digging deeper.

"And the bitches?" Aaron knew Jeff was referring to the secrets in the mini box.

Aaron exhaled. "Those bitches I used to fuck with on tour with the artists. It didn't mean shit, and bitches knew that. I kept it a hunnit."

"Might have made one of them fall in love, perhaps?"

"They wouldn't know who I'm plugged with who invests in HEAT."

"Women could win an Oscar award for being a detective when it comes down to some dick that got them feeling some type away. Know what I mean?" Tyler suggested.

Aaron rubbed his chin as his father emerged, front and center of his thoughts.

"Yo, son, these young cats are right. Who was the bitch that ran up the stairs while you were talking to the boss in Tucson?"

Tyler waved his hand in front of Aaron's face.

"What's up, Aaron? What you are thinking, and don't hold out," Jeff said, hands pressed against the island where Aaron and Tyler sat.

"I went to see the owner of the mall Outlets on Scottsdale Road in Tucson today."

"And?" Jeff asked impatiently.

"I kicked it with her about giving me some time to replace the lost money from one of the investors pulling out from the company. I was officially ready to open, and now I have to postpone."

"Damn cuz, you know all the upcoming new artists, and you know one of the major owners of the Outlets? I'd invest in HEAT." Tyler gave Aaron some dap.

Aaron knew of Tyler's wealthy freelance businesses in Las Vegas and Detroit and replied. "We can talk, bro."

Jeff continued his investigation.

"What did she say to you after you told her you needed more time?"

"She said I should think about relocating." Aaron disagreed with what his boss said, then continued, "I should take this time as a learning experience so my next store, I could run more appropriately. She gave me tips on assets, liabilities, and payroll, introduced me to Dave Ramsey, saying I need to continue educating myself on money, building my wealth, and keeping it."

Jeff listened attentively.

"That's sound advice," Tyler protested.

''She doesn't find you fit in your ability to run your business, big homie," Jeff announced as he attempted to connect the dots to the investigation he called "lightweight."

What Jeff had just said bruised Aaron's ego because he hadn't thought about what she said in the way Jeff interpreted it.

"Was that all, fam?" Jeff asked.

Aaron fell into deep thought, and Tyler interrupted.

"Don't hold back. "

Aaron procrastinated by taking a swig of water. "There was a bitch there." Aaron studied his thoughts. "The boss lady got a daughter." His Jersey accent was reinforced when he became agitated. "I'd never met or seen pictures of her, and my focus was soaking up info that helped my business and getting some pussy so I didn't care about meeting her kid. But the bitch there looked familiar, yo, her name even."

"Looks like that Lupe girl, son." Aaron's father spoke from his intuition.

Aaron had seen Claudia's daughter rush up some stairs at a distance in the Tucson estate but couldn't determine if it was Lupe. He thought that Guadalupe and Lupe had to be the same name, just different versions.

"But it couldn't be her," Aaron thought aloud.

Aaron looked at his Apple wristwatch, which read ten o'clock. He wondered about the time he had known Lupe, which was a few months. They'd been on a couple of dates. He thought about their first date at the Breakfast Spot. They got to know one another. She explained that she was from Mexico. Nowhere specific. She snuck across the

US border when she was eighteen years old. She came to Arizona to work for her family's restaurant, to make a new life for herself. She struggled to get where she wanted to because she gave her family money for room, board, and other needs. Initially, after they had met, he would pick her up from 19th Ave and Cactus. She never invited him into her and her family's home. So there had been no way to fact-check who she was. Realizing the likeliness that she had been playing him all along, Aaron sat alert. He needed some answers, and a part of him felt like Lupe was the root of it all.

"I'll be back," Aaron announced, then he jumped up from his chair and quickly went to the door, throwing on his off-white and cream Jordan 11s and rushing to his car.

"Where is he going?" Tyler asked Jeff, confused.

"He's probably about to find out who's been trying to get at him. I'm-a follow him. You stay here with Faith," Jeff ordered.

Chapter Thirteen

Aaron did eighty up the I17 to get to Lupe's family house, and something in him knew it was her at the estate. After Aaron's speeding slowed because of morning traffic, he reminisced about every occasion with Lupe. Something didn't feel right to him.

Aaron called Lupe.

"Hello?" she answered, sounding like she had just awakened.

"Where you at? I gotta kick it with you!" Aaron screamed.

"It's ten o'clock in the morning, and I'm sleeping," Lupe lied into the phone.

"Get ya ass up! I said we need to talk asap!" Aaron barked, and Lupe knew something was up.

"All right, all right, give me an hour to wake up and get going."

"Get the fuck up now, be at the Breakfast Spot."

Lupe began to pace the floor as thoughts went through her head. As the thoughts traveled through her brain, she walked the plush carpet of her bedroom and stared down at her freshly painted jeweled nails.

"If Aaron knows..." Lupe paused and shook her head to shake off the thought. "My father would have warned me."

Lupe knew her father was usually one step ahead of his enemies and hadn't failed at conquering a discrepancy. To be sure, she called her father and asked what was up. Lupe's father reassured her everything was fine and that he would be around. She decided to continue to play her role. Lupe quickly dressed, jumped into her Nissan Maxima, and drove to where she and Aaron would have breakfast and talk about business for the day.

Aaron stood outside the restaurant, looking like he had just left the bed. Lupe found Aaron's wardrobe peculiar. She took in his simple attire, a V-neck white t-shirt, cream Jordan basketball shorts, and Jordan 11s. She was stunned that Aaron came out in public dressed this way. Aaron was very particular about his appearance and wouldn't be caught on the streets dressed like a teenage boy.

"Hey," Lupe said suspiciously as Aaron stood in front of the restaurant with a skeptical look.

"Where the fuck were you yesterday at four-thirty in the afternoon?" Aaron skipped the introductions and got straight to the point.

"I was..." Lupe flinched from Aaron's irate behavior.

"Don't lie to me. Before coming here, I went by your family house and was told you don't live there."

Lupe was stunned and lost for words. She felt some comfort when she spotted Teko and Sam in an SUV at a deli shop near the Breakfast Spot.

***

Brazo had instructed Teko and Sam to follow Lupe and keep tabs on her interaction with Aaron.

Teko's face returned a menacing gaze in Aaron and Lupe's direction. His trigger finger twitched, ready to end Aaron's life as he watched the exchange between Aaron and Lupe. Teko thought if he ended him now, Aaron's irate behavior toward Brazo's daughter would be his excuse. He knew Brazo got soft on him. Back in the day, they would have beaten Aaron as he begged for his life, and they would have quickly taken whatever Aaron had that they wanted. He never knew his boss to play these kinds of games.

Teko could feel Sam looking at him and decided not to walk over and break up the exchange between Aaron and Lupe.

***

"What the hell is going on?" Jeff shouted as he watched the confrontation unfold from a deli shop across from the Breakfast Spot.

"So, he got another bitch, and who are these Mexican niggas?" Jeff looked through his dark-shaded Ray Bans as he watched Teko return to the SUV with tinted windows.

"Dwayne Johnson-looking nigga looked like he was about to get at Aaron."

Jeff watched Teko and Sam sit in the car as Aaron in Lupe continued their talk.

Aaron's phone rang, and Jeff could hear the iPhone ringtone from the deli shop.

***

"Money calling," Aaron said as he looked at his phone and back at Lupe. Lupe knew it was her father contacting Aaron. She could only imagine Teko telling her father Aaron had disrespected her and wanting to set him straight.

"No, you said you were out," Lupe objected to Aaron's idea to get the money together. She knew her father was on the other side of that phone call and felt afraid for Aaron.

Simultaneously, Aaron felt Lupe was connected to whoever threatened him and Faith and wanted to know for sure.

"No, we're going to get this money!" Aaron barked loudly, startling a lady who walked past to get into the Breakfast Spot.

"Where at?" Lupe asked, frustrated as she was becoming impatient with his behavior. Although she loved him, she never tolerated disrespect from any man. He acted crazier when he was sobering from Midazolam and cannabis.

Whatever Aaron had coming to him, he deserved. She grew tired of his arrogant, rah-rah behavior.

"Funny, Sunny Home," Aaron answered Lupe sarcastically.

Aaron got into his car and pulled off, with Lupe tailing him. Soon after, the black-tinted SUV followed closely behind Lupe.

"Lightweight," Jeff confirmed as he watched the ordeal happen.

***

Lupe and Aaron walked into the hotel suite in Scottsdale. Lupe sat her Victoria's Secret duffle bag onto the suite's king-sized bed.

Aaron watched her every move closely as he tightly held his fully loaded semi-automatic pistol.

He sat at the desk in the room, and his father began to show himself again front and center in his mind.

"You want a drink?" Lupe asked.

Lupe could sense the tension with Aaron. "I need one." She spoke as if disgusted with the business she and Aaron had together.

"Don't drink anything from that snake, son. She almost got rid of me forever with the last cocktail she gave you," Aaron's father said as he skimmed through a Vanity Fair magazine.

"I'm good," Aaron answered intuitively. "I'm going to watch you fuck when the customer gets here."

Lupe looked at Aaron, stunned, thinking today was the end of her connection with him.

She couldn't drug Aaron, making him fall asleep because he refused to have a drink. Lupe would usually mix Midazolam with cognac.

Things were going down differently that afternoon, and Lupe and Aaron knew it.

Lupe began to panic because her father had coached her on putting Aaron to sleep and giving him the money once he woke up. This moment was different, so she went into the bathroom and texted Teko to ask what she should do because he refused to drink. Teko texted that he would come up to the suite to follow through with their staged prostitution until Brazo got there. Teko and Sam were already in the parking lot waiting for Brazo to arrive.

"You gone get dressed?" Aaron asked, knocking on the bathroom door.

Lupe walked out of the bathroom naked.

"Dressed." Aaron stared at her in awe of her perfected gym body.

"Just kidding," Lupe said to ease her and Aaron's anxieties. She put on a Victoria's Secret panty and bra set from her bag.

Teko knocked at the door, and Aaron went into the bathroom.

"I'll give you a little privacy," he said as he closed the door.

Teko walked in, and Lupe looked at the bathroom door to indicate that Aaron was there.

"Four thousand dollars." Lupe held her hand out to Teko and took him by surprise.

Teko pulled out all his money from his pocket, knowing he had nothing close to four thousand dollars. He forgot she was "prostituting" on the secret app that only A/B-class celebrities, business-oriented, and people of a specific caliber had access to. Teko pulled out two thousand dollars. Aaron spotted the money through the cracked bathroom door, knowing the payment wasn't nearly enough for the client's requested services.

"Aye, B, that's not all the money." Aaron snatched the bills from Teko's hand, sending Teko's patience out the window.

Teko pulled two guns from his waist. Aaron raised his hands, immediately regretting leaving his pistol on the desk.

"Get dressed," Teko ordered, and Lupe rushed to pull her dress over her body.

"Yo, you know this nigga?" Aaron asked Lupe. Lupe didn't answer.

"You know this nigga!" Aaron restated, answering his own question.

"Fuck is you, and why are you sending threats?" Aaron looked Teko in the eye.

Teko contemplated whether to blow Aaron's brains out in front of Lupe.

"Shut up," Teko said casually. "Or I'm about to put you to sleep for good."

Sam walked into the suite and said, "Brazo just made it here and is on his way up."

Aaron looked at Lupe in disbelief, and Lupe stared back with a *forgive me* look, mouthing the words *I'm sorry.*

Teko didn't hear a word Sam said because all he could think about was ending Aaron.

Teko cocked his guns, ready to shoot. Aaron noticed a red light on Teko's chest. Once Teko began to pull the trigger, he was blown back by a shot that pierced through the window, sending him flying back into the wall. Before Sam could shoot, he joined Teko in passing back into the wall.

The bullets pierced the window making a shattering sound. Aaron shielded his body with an arm as glass flew in all directions inside the suite. The echo of Sam and Teko's bodies flying into the wall sent chills down Aaron's body. Aaron was in shock as he watched Teko and Sam hang their heads to the side with blood spilling from their mouths.

Lupe let a shrilling cry as she thought she was next on the anonymous shooter's list.

Aaron grabbed his gun and went for the stair exit, leaving Lupe, Teko, and Sam behind.

At the exit was a black-tinted Trailblazer SS that drove up on him and knew he was about to die. The window came down.

"Nigga get in the car!" Jeff screamed like a madman. Jeff drove through traffic to get back to the condo. Aaron realized Jeff had been following him and felt relieved that he did.

"Who were them niggas?" Jeff questioned.

"Bro, I don't know, but the bitch I was tricking with do."

Jeff gave Aaron a look that made the hairs on Aaron's neck stand up. If looks could kill, Aaron would be dead.

Aaron continued to think while Jeff raced through traffic.

"Yo, that was the bitch at my boss's house in Tucson. Lupe's mom is my boss, yo." Aaron realized and became irate, sending his blood pressure and cranial nerves bulging on his forehead.

"Boss lady is affiliated with the setup," Jeff suggested, then his eyes widened and his nonchalant stance dissipated. "Aye fam, those niggas are here?" Jeff questioned, confused as he stared at the SUV parked outside Aaron's home.

Chapter Fourteen

Sunny Home's Hotel and Resort was a five-minute drive from Aaron and Faith's condo. After Brazo heard the first shot, his selfish tendencies overtook him. He left his friends and daughter behind. He thought they were all dead by the sound of the shots fired and people running frantically through the hotel. He didn't want to get caught by the police so he let the one he thought was the killer run free. Brazo knew the cost of playing this violent game he had played for so long. Loved ones such as daughters could get caught up in the crossfire between opponents. He wanted to get to Faith first.

Aaron and Jeff reached the widely opened condo door. They were shocked as Tyler stood there with two pistols pointed at Brazo, who stood with his hands around Faith's neck and gun pointed at her head.

"Fam, I went to get Faith something to eat while she showered, and he was here when I got back," Tyler explained to Jeff, who had the look of a killer in his eyes.

"My cousin ain't got shit to do with what you and Aaron got going on, Boss." Tyler began to plead with an angry Brazo as Faith began to cry hysterically.

Teko and Sam look-alikes entered the condo entrance with guns cocked. Brazo had called for backup after hearing the gunshots fire at the hotel.

"You took my spot at the Outlets, you fucked my daughter, and you fucked my wife." Brazo squeezed the back of Faith's neck tighter.

Aaron walked closer, and Brazo pointed the gun at Aaron.

"One more step and your entire family dies today." Brazo said with authority. "I'm trying to live right and do business with fewer dead bodies. Aaron comes along and questions the changed man I'm trying to be." Brazo shifted to a calm demeanor in an instant. His personality often changed from calm to killer and back again when necessary. Everyone looked at Brazo, wondering what he was up to. Brazo repeated, "You fucked my wife."

"I didn't know Lupe was your wife." Aaron tried to console his hurt enemy.

"Lupe's my daughter, who you fucked too. My wife Claudia left me because of you. She shared my pussy, money, and knowledge with you, and now it's time for you to pay up. Where's the money I gave you?"

Aaron looked confused.

"Oh, you thought you were making money by having my daughter prostitute?"

Realization dawned in Aaron's eyes. "Alright, I'll give you the money back. Don't hurt Faith." Aaron went to the linen closet and brought out a shoe box full of neatly rubber-banded stacks of cash.

Tyler looked at Jeff with pleading eyes as if to ask what to do. Jeff winked at Tyler to ease his worries, and Tyler knew instantly Jeff had something up his sleeve.

"Good boy." Brazo congratulated Aaron on bringing him the money.

"There is a document with the conditions of our agreement." Brazo gestured with his gun toward the kitchen island. "You will sign it. I will close your ridiculous store. You will stay far away from the Outlets of Scottsdale Road, any Maricopa property, and my family. If you don't, I will kill you. I suggest you don't take my threats lightly." As an afterthought, he said, "She fell in love. And thought she could live without me," Brazo spoke with sorrow in his throat. "Well, she and you will pay. Bring her in, fellas." Brazo's men brought in a tied-up woman who screamed through her taped mouth.

"Shut up!" Brazo screamed at her.

One of Brazo's men dumped the woman onto the couch in front of Aaron.

"Maybe I'll fuck your pregnant whore." Brazo let out an evil smile. "They say pregnant pussy is the best pussy."

Aaron looked at the woman who was Claudia. She also was his boss, ex-lover, and one of the biggest investors of the Outlets of Scottsdale Road. The woman who listened to his dreams and supported him every step of the way. She helped finance his store. Aaron was twenty-eight when they met, and he had never been into older women. But she was refined and experienced in every way. Claudia taught him everything he needed to know about being an entrepreneur. Although she was fifteen years older than Aaron, she was what he needed to achieve his dreams. He would always be thankful for that.

He looked between the two women who meant the world to him and questioned his loyalty. His father emerged from his thoughts, making him have the urge to protect his unborn that Faith carried.

Whether he was at his best or worst, Faith was there for him despite what he went through with a smile and a sincere heart.

"You gone have to kill me, bra. Take yo wife and let my girl go."

Tyler was hurt, showing emotion. "You a greedy muthafucka!" He was furious at the ultimatum given to Aaron. "He fucked your wife and daughter, so what? You should have kept them hoes on a leash!"

"You think you can disrespect me too?" More of Brazo's men came on cue, outnumbering Aaron and his family. One of Brazo's men punched Tyler in the face for his comment.

Tyler laughed, saying, "Nigga you hit like a bitch!" Brazo's man cocked his gun at Tyler, shooting him.

"Freeze! Get on the ground." To Aaron's surprise, some of Brazo's men who showed up were part of the Federal Bureau of Investigations. He noticed this as more men swarmed in wearing vests with the FBI logo stitched on them.

"No!" Faith yelled in disbelief that someone shot Tyler.

Jeff began examining Tyler to make sure the shot wasn't fatal. "Fam, get up," Jeff pleaded. "Get a fucking EMT in here!" he screamed into the phone as the other FBI agents rounded up Brazo's men.

"Tyler, get up, cuz." Jeff stared down at Tyler.

"Bro, you a fucking cop?" Tyler grimaced in pain at the fact that his cousin was really an FBI agent.

Tyler could see the desperation in Jeff's eyes as the EMTs came to his aid.

"He shot me in the arm." Tyler grabbed his arm and groaned in pain. "Nigga was hating on the biceps."

Tyler's joke calmed Jeff's anxiety.

"Bro, am I delusional? I'm going crazy," Tyler complained.

"My nigga what's up? What's wrong?" Jeff cried out to Tyler.

"Nigga you a cop!"

With an exaggerated smile, Jeff shook his head. "Surprise." Jeff lifted his shirt to show his FBI logo bulletproof vest. "Had to cut a deal with the pigs years ago."

"But why is that a secret, fam? That's good, Jeff. I'm actually proud of you."

"Yeah. All the rumors you hear about me ain't true. I protect the hood, fam. I ain't just murking niggas," Jeff confidently said. "Unless niggas like Brazo provoke me."

Tyler looked at Jeff as if he was lying.

Jeff winked at Tyler as the EMT accompanied Tyler with his bleeding arm. Jeff could read the skepticism in Tyler's eyes and knew he would be in for a long talk over some broccoli and tequila.

***

Brazo yelled at Aaron as he was being detained and pulled out of the condo. "You took everything from me, and now your bastard baby is mine!"

Faith hunched over, grabbing her stomach and back with tears filling her eyes.

She let out an agonizing scream, piercing the ears of everyone still standing in the room. During the hassle of prying Brazo from Faith, Brazo had kicked her in the back as hard as possible.

"She won't make it," Brazo exclaimed.

Faith fainted from panting.

Brazo let out a laugh.

"Get him the fuck out of here. Why was he still here?" Jeff thundered.

Aaron looked at the situation unfolding in confusion, then snapped out of it.

He followed Jeff to the door of the apartment as Jeff shouted at a cursing Brazo, who was still trying to wrestle away from the police. It was no use since two officers were flanked at his sides and his hands were cuffed behind his back.

"Drug trafficking, you attempted to shoot an FBI agent, and now a rape attempt? Mr. Brazo, you're racking up some charges," one of the agents announced. The agent shook his head and began again.

"I'm sure this one didn't come here of own free will," he said, referring to the tied-up Claudia. He began to untie and remove the tape from her mouth.

"Your ass is mine now," Jeff said, with a grin.

Aaron was dazed for another second before he snapped out of it and ran over to Faith.

"Get my cousin to the hospital now!" Jeff yelled.

"Hold on, baby, just hold on," Aaron pleaded.

Aaron and Jeff rushed behind EMT, following them to the hospital.

***

"Aye, we need to talk, fam." Jeff asked Aaron as Jeff pushed his SUV through the Arizona traffic behind the EMT,

Aaron hesitantly replied to Jeff with a look of humiliation on his face. "What's up?" Aaron's voice cracked as he looked at Jeff's badge with disbelief.

"Nigga yeah, I'm the feds. You got some secret dealings you gotta be straight up with me about, or you're going to see the inside of a prison for a couple of years." Jeff chastised as he looked at the ambulance before him, flushed from this ordeal.

Aaron got the hint as he looked at ambulance too and then back at Jeff as he hurried through traffic.

"Damn, man," Aaron said under his breath as he searched his brain for answers.

Aaron had questions and thoughts running through his mind at a hundred miles per hour. He wondered how Jeff knew about his secret dealings. Also, exactly how much did he know?

Jeff explained. "I can finesse guns and money. But all this other shit you got going on, attempting to prostitute, bro...." Jeff paused as he looked Aaron in his eyes and shook his head, saying, "I don't know, bro." He stared into Aaron's eyes. "Faith, Tyler, and I didn't have our fathers growing up." Jeff stared back into traffic. "I would hate to see Faith raise a child without you, and then we got another fatherless child lost in this world."

Aaron listened as he looked at the blaring sirens coming from the EMT vehicle in front of them, concerned.

"Nah, man I understand."

Chapter Fifteen

J eff, Tyler, and Aaron sat outside Faith's emergency room door as doctors and nurses worked quickly on her.

After an hour of heated arguments with the emergency room manager, all three men finally sat.

The doctor arrived. "Faith was heavily sedated. We had to get the fetus out of her, or she would have died. She fought with us, begging to keep the fetus, so I hope you men will support her loss."

***

A nurse arrived in Faith's room. "Hi, I'm Jeremy. I have come to take you to the observation unit." His cheery voice woke Faith up.

"Jeremy?" Faith rose her head from the hospital bed's pillow. "We worked together. You trained me on contract when I arrived at this hospital to work." Faith was hardly able to get her words out.

"Now I'm here to care for you the next few days." Jeremy smiled and took Faith's hand into his. "You know the protocol. I will ask you some silly questions I ask everyone before we leave the ER and head up to observation. I know it's you, but just in case someone is listening," Jeremy said with a wink.

"Please tell me your name, date of birth, where you are, and why?"

"Faith Cannon, July 13, 1991, I'm at the hospital," Faith said through tears.

Jeremy gave her tissues.

"Hey, you did great. I'm sorry if I was being pushy, and it's okay."

Jeremy enclosed Faith's hand into his as if to say *you're in great hands.*

Jeremy began to type Faith's responses into the ER room computer.

***

Aaron grew angry as he thought about not being there for Faith more than he was and seeing someone care for Faith as Jeremy was.

"Yo, who the fuck are you? Another nurse said she was taking her to observation. You don't look like Nurse Annie to me." Sweat saturated Aaron's t-shirt from blasting his words.

"Sir, let me get you some water. I'm Jeremy, Faith's nurse, and I'm here to take her to observation. You can tag along if you'd like. I'll go and get that water and be back in five," Jeremy said with a smile, leaving Faith and Aaron alone.

"Are you okay, Aaron? You've been strange these last few weeks and haven't been yourself. You don't look good now," Faith said.

Aaron kissed Faith, hanging his body close to hers as he spoke with a heavy heart.

"Look, Faith. I'm learning as I go, and life's a bitch." Aaron shook his head as he thought of the trials and tribulations he had been through and conquered and the ones that had been unraveling in his life lately.

Faith stared as if she was waiting for further explanation, so he continued.

"I didn't have my father in my life. I wouldn't have made many mistakes if I had someone there to teach me how to be a man," Aaron confessed, feeling a heavy weight lift off his shoulders and his father in his mind.

Faith felt there was no excuse for how he had been treating her but didn't have enough strength to fight him, so she nodded in resignation.

"But what happened to you?" Aaron asked and paused as he looked down at her abdomen. "I mean, the baby," he whispered.

"The baby was unattached from my uterus, and there was too much bleeding."

For the first time in a long time, Aaron focused on Faith's feelings rather than his own. "I'm sorry this happened to you. But just to let you know, I would have never left you stuck, Ma. I would have come through for you and the baby." Tears filled his eyes as he spoke.

"What do you mean, Aaron?" Faith asked through yawns.

At first, Faith's yawning at his tears made Aaron tense up, then he remembered that she was sedated and shook it off. He explained. "Meaning, I do love you. I won't be like my father and leave you stuck. We might not always get along, but I got you, Ma." Aaron's tone was filled with sincerity as he spoke to Faith.

Faith couldn't converse any longer with Aaron without falling asleep.

***

Aaron couldn't fathom seeing Faith like this and walked outside the room where Jeff and Tyler sat. Tyler quickly got up, practically knocking over Aaron to get into Faith's room. Before Aaron could join Jeff where he sat, suddenly, the news caught his attention as he looked over his shoulders, thoughts interrupted by the blaring television in a patient's room he was passing by.

"The victims at the shooting scene in North Scottsdale are alive but in critical condition and headed to the nearest hospital." The news anchor said, reminding Aaron of Lupe's horrific reaction to Teko and Sam's bodies being forced into the hotel room's wall by the piercing bullets.

Aaron suddenly felt a hand touch his shoulders, invading his thoughts.

"Let me explain," Lupe announced breathlessly.

Aaron blinked in surprise because he hadn't even seen her approach him. He stared back and forth between the tv screen and Lupe. His fists balled at his sides, but he wouldn't dare try to hit her in front of Jeff.

Still, he couldn't help but feel hatred toward Lupe because she set him up, and her father was the reason he and Faith lost their baby.

Still, he listened to her explanation.

Lupe pushed the hair from in front of her face and put it behind her ear while looking down. She couldn't seem to get any words out as she rattled her brain to come clean to Aaron. She couldn't look him in his eyes.

After a few moments of frustrating silence, Aaron spoke. "There's nothing you can say, Lupe."

"But...."

"But what?" Aaron sucked his teeth and continued. "Look, I gotta figure some shit out, and if you can't talk, keep it moving Ma."

"I never meant for this to happen this way. My father made me do it," Lupe pleaded, looking up at Aaron with tears in her eyes.

"You set me up and put me in danger."

"Aaron, I love you and will do anything to make this right."

"You clearly don't know what love is, Lupe. I did nothing wrong, yet you tried to deceive me."

Aaron turned his back to Lupe and began to walk away.

Jeff opened his mouth as if he was going to say something but closed it.

"Wait," Lupe said as she reached out to grab his arm to keep him from leaving.

"Lupe, we are done."

***

Jeff rolled his eyes at Aaron's mishaps. Aaron was gone for ten minutes before he rejoined Jeff and Tyler, who had emerged from Faith's room after Lupe left in tears.

"Fam, I can't leave Faith like this. She's hurt." Aaron pleaded because he knew he might face jail for his secret business affairs with Lupe and the escorting app. He thought he was accessing it off-grid but somehow wasn't if Jeff knew about it.

"Fam, off the record, why did you do it?" Jeff put the tips of his prayer hands together, touching his chin as he questioned Aaron.

"I have a daughter."

Jeff looked at Aaron, shocked because he didn't know about his other child.

"When my fashion shit took off, my daughter's mother in Florida found out about it and then threatened to go to court." Aaron pinched the crease of his eyes to wipe away growing tension. "Faith got pregnant and went on bed rest, so I tended to her needs. I stopped seeing my daughter for like two weeks. My daughter's mother threatened me with child support, so I had to make some money. I got past the debt I was trying to get rid of. Shit has been like a domino effect. I'm just trying to get ahead."

As the conversation continued, Aaron's mind was invaded by his father's visit.

"Although this situation is heavy, son, see what deal Jeff has to offer."

"I'll figure out something, fam," Jeff nodded as if to say *I got you.* "But only on one condition."

"Anything, bro," Aaron said without hesitation.

"You keep away from my cousin. You got some shit you need to deal with."

"I got you." Aaron was surprised at Jeff's kind gesture but began thinking of a plan to rehabilitate himself.

"I mean now," Jeff said sternly. "There's no baby and no reason for you to stay."

As Aaron turned to leave, he began to think about the events that brought him to this point in his life. Aaron couldn't shake the feeling of being watched, so he kept looking over his shoulder. He couldn't help but wonder how Jeff would plan to get him out of the situation he saw no way out of. But he began to mentally prepare himself for it all. He knew it was risky what Jeff promised him, but he had to trust him. He had to believe everything would work out in the end because if it did, he could smooth things over with Faith and be a better father than the one chained to his mind. It was over, but he felt things weren't quite the end.

To be continued...

Dear Reader,

This story ends at a cliffhanger, but it is far from over, as Aaron thought. Will he pull himself together to be the man Faith needs, or is their relationship over for good? Will Lupe come back into the picture, or are her and Aaron really over?

Lastly, Teko and Sam are still alive, per the news report. Will they come back with a vengeance, or hide in the shadows, licking their wounds?

Find out in part two.

Made in the USA
Middletown, DE
05 July 2023

34598467R00080